SC

– a new publishing i̲n̲ ̲...̲ ̲g̲ ̲y̲...̲ ̲t̲h̲e̲ ̲v̲e̲r̲y̲ ̲b̲e̲s̲t̲ in adventure SF. Time travel, galactic empires, alien invasions – all the traditional elements that have made science fiction the most exciting form of literature of the 20th century. In Venture SF, we'll be bringing you novels of action adventure – no short stories, no fantasy, no boredom. If action adventure SF is your type of reading, then Venture SF is for you – every book published by us will be the first appearance in paperback in the UK. Start collecting them now!

VENTURE SCIENCE FICTION SERIES

Series editors Rog Peyton and Rod Milner

VENTURE
SCIENCE FICTION

The Sky is Filled with Ships

RICHARD C. MEREDITH

ARROW BOOKS
VENTURE SF

Arrow Books Limited
62-65 Chandos Place, London WC2N 4NW

An imprint of Century Hutchinson Limited

London Melbourne Sydney Auckland
Johannesburg and agencies throughout
the world

First published in 1969 by Ballantine Books, Inc., USA
First published in Great Britain in 1988 by Arrow Books

Printed and bound in Great Britain by
Anchor Brendon Limited, Tiptree, Essex

ISBN 0 09 061860 5

To my wife, Joy

Chapter 1

He had never seen the Lunar terminals so crowded nor had he ever seen the crowds so quiet. Here on Luna things still looked normal; there were no signs of bombing, the terminal staff and their automated equipment still functioned normally. There was, he noticed, an unusually large number of soldiers, though few were part of the sullen, milling crowd. Most stood armed and silent, dressed in Federation combat green, their backs against the walls, their faces impassive.

But the people—he could see it in their faces, fear just below the level of panic. Many of them were refugees, as he was in a sense, just come to Luna from the star worlds. They knew what was happening *Out There* and what could be happening here soon—and they were frightened.

He turned and looked out through the transparent bubble that covered this section of the huge, sprawling Lunar terminal. Stark, harsh shadows fell across the spaceport, slowly, imperceptibly lengthening as Luna's backside swung toward the sun. Out there, in the near vacuum of the moon's surface, glittering in the brilliant late afternoon sunlight, lay the starship that had carried him from Odin back to Earth's companion. It lay quiet and still now, like some huge, metallic sea beast thrown up on this uninviting shore by a terrible storm, on the southern edge

1

of Mare Serenitatis, this misnamed Sea of Serenity. He wondered if that great beast would ever again swim in the oceans of space, and he doubted it.

Captain Robert L. Janas of the Solar Trading Company, of late Acting Manager of the STC Odin Major Terminal, before that commander of the STCSS *President Regan,* Terran by birth, starman by occupation, looked up at the moon's pitch-black sky and saw the brilliant half-Earth hanging like a painted toy against star-spangled velvet.

She's been lucky so far, he told himself, but now her luck's run out. He muttered something that was halfway between a curse and a prayer and was about to turn away when a glint of climbing light caught his eye.

One following another until there were dozens of them, moving spots of reflected sunlight, a fleet, no, an armada of starships, rose into the Lunar sky from somewhere far across the flat plains of Mare Serenitatis. He knew what ships they were, and he knew their names and their purpose. A chill ran down his spine. He ticked off those names as they rose skyward, fell into orbit around Luna, and waited for their companions. Out there, moving starward now, were *Marathon* and *Belleau Wood, Bull Run* and *Agincourt;* one was *Salamis* and one was *Argonne Forest,* and there was *Pork Chop Hill* and *Waterloo* and others with names as vivid. Climbing away from Luna were the cream of the space fleets of the Terran Federation, the greatest of the heavy battle cruisers of the stars.

And soon, Janas knew, rendezvousing with them, lifting from other Lunar ports, would be the Federation's destroyer fleets, ships named *North Carolina* and *Revenge, Victory* and *Bismarck, Royal William* and *Hood, Yamato* and *Alabama,* and a hundred more.

Together they would meet in orbit around Luna, and with others they would climb away, moving starward, and somewhere in the darkness between stars, somewhere in the grayness of another universe, they would meet that other fleet, a fleet whose ships bore names like their own, manned by men like themselves, and the battle would be joined; the Great Rebellion would reach its climax. And then?

Janas tore his eyes away from the sky, wondering what it would be like here a month from now. Would the Lunar terminals still be operating? Would they even exist? Whose ships would be in her dark sky? And what of Earth herself? Will she be green and blue still, or will her continents, like those of Antigone, be shrouded in smoke and her oceans covered with steam?

Robert L. Janas, Captain, Solar Trading Company, was halfway between birth and death according to the actuary tables of this, the year 979 of the Federation, or the year 3483 on the old calendar. He was a tall man with a café au lait complexion, unusual for a person born in the section of North America from which he had come, but his mother's people had been bred by the mingled races of the plains of Asia, and her blood ran thick in his veins. His face was made of sharp angles and harsh lines, a quickly wrought sketch of a medieval knight; few women called him handsome but none had called him ugly. His eyes were deep set and dark, the eyes of a man accustomed to peering into the endless depths of space, the eyes of a dreamer strangely set into the face of a warrior, and perhaps this is why something in his appearance harked back to the days of steel armor, broadswords and towering castles. The darkness of his hair was shot with a premature gray that made him look older than he was. When he walked there was a slight though noticeable limp; a scar and a transplanted trochanter were the only reminders of a fight on an alien world so far away and so long ago that he hardly remembered it. The blue and gold uniform he wore looked well on him, for Robert Janas was every inch a starship captain.

But now, in this year 979 FE, standing on the surface of Luna and watching the fleets of the Federation move toward the stars, Janas felt little of the feline strength that resided in his slender body, felt little more than a cold apprehension. The end was near, the "Imperium" was about to die, mankind would be plunged into the darkest of dark ages, and there was nothing that could be done to stop it.

Shifting his attaché case from his left hand to his right he walked away from the observation deck and back toward the center of the terminal dome. Rising from the tiled floor of the dome were the information and reservation desks, forming a circle around the reservation computer input station, which was strangely quiet and still as it had never been before. Above the input unit was a pedestal on which sat a 3-V tank, and in the depths of the tank was a pleasant looking young man seated behind a broad desk. Before him were several sheets of paper that he shuffled, perhaps nervously; behind him on the wall was a Mercator projection of Earth, emblazoned with the combined letters "T" and "F" of the Federation. The young man was speaking.

". . . after weeks of discussion. Citizen Herrera, Chairman of the Federation, announced within the hour that Citizen Altho Franken, President of the

Solar Trading Company, has agreed to allow the use of STC ships and personnel in the defense of Federation territory against the rebel Kantralas."

The face of the young newscaster faded away to be replaced by the pudgy-faced, hard-eyed image of the Chairman of the Terran Federation, Citizen Jonal Constantine Herrera. The word "prerecorded" appeared in the lower right hand corner of the 3-V tank. The image spoke, the words heavily flavored with the east European dialect of his childhood: "The noble and self-sacrificing action of Citizen Altho Franken will long be remembered by the peoples of the Federation. We all know the Solar Trading Company's long standing neutrality in political affairs, and we can appreciate Citizen Franken's hesitation to break such a time-honored tradition. However, my fellow citizens, it well may be that Citizen Franken's actions of today will go down in history as the turning point of our long, hard battle to maintain the integrity of the Federation."

As Herrera's image faded the face and voice of the newscaster returned. "Chairman Herrera went on to say that . . ."

Violently Janas turned away from the 3-V tank, the sinking feeling in his stomach threatening to carry him to his knees. That fool, he yelled silently to himself, that goddamned fool!

He found a place to sit and collect his thoughts. Opening his attaché case he took out typewritten copies of the reports that were his reason for being on Luna, his reason for coming across the long light-years to Earth—to deliver those reports about the star worlds and the rebel forces to Altho Franken. Franken, once Janas had informed him of their existence, had asked to see them, had asked Janas to return to

Earth, to give his opinions about the war's probable outcome, and had said that he would make no final decision about the STC's stand during the imminent battles until he had seen the reports and talked with Janas. But now, after Janas had crossed light-years and stood some 384,000 kilometers from Earth, Franken had broken his promise and committed the future of the STC into the hands of the TF Chairman, Jonal Herrera. A few more hours, that was all he need have waited, and Janas could have spoken with him—and perhaps prevented the destruction of *all* of civilization.

Janas slipped the papers back into the attaché case and angrily slammed it shut, wishing that the feeling in his stomach would go away.

"Paging Captain Robert Janas," said a voice from the ring of loudspeakers that decorated the 3-V's supporting column. "Captain Robert Janas, please come to the Solar Trading Company reservation desks in terminal dome A-3."

There was a moment of silence before the pleasantly feminine voice repeated the message.

With infinite weariness Janas rose and crossed the tiled floor to the circle of desks. The girl sitting behind the desk he approached was wearing an unusually revealing dress, though by the cut and colors of it he knew it to be a regulation STC uniform. Apparently there had been some changes on Earth since he had last been there. The girl smiled.

"I'm Robert Janas."

"Good afternoon, captain," she said. "There is an analogue call from Earth for you. Would you take it in booth twelve, please," and she pointed to the row of analogue communications booths near the corridor that connected this dome with the main terminal building.

"Thank you," Janas replied, and turned away toward the booths.

A few minutes later, sitting in a plush chair that faced a seemingly blank wall, Janas glanced briefly at the two small consoles that bracketed him. On his right was the communications unit, a handful of controls to adjust the "picture" and sound that would spring to life as soon as he waved his hand over a certain photocell. The console on his left was an auto-bartender and was, at that moment, a welcome sight. Janas dropped a coin into the slot, punched a button, then waited until a panel slid aside and a tall, chilled glass of Brajen whiskey rose to meet his hand. Thus fortified he covered the photocell with his palm.

He had not bothered to wonder who was calling him all the way from Earth. Enid did not know that he was coming in on this particular flight; only two people did know, and he did not think that one of them, Citizen Altho Franken, would feel any need to call him *now*.

The wall before him shimmered for a moment then became transparent. The effect was that of looking through into another room that seemed to be separated from his by only a thin sheet of paraglas. The other room was of approximately the same size, though more luxurious, and the opposite wall was emblazoned with a stylized representation of a solar disk and rays, the symbol of the Solar Trading Company.

Sitting two meters away, so Janas' eyes told him, was a short, stocky man, fair-skinned and carrot-haired, and perhaps a decade or so his junior. Only the light-speed delay betrayed the image's unreality.

When Janas keyed the analogue transmitter, half a hundred scanners had recorded three dimensional images of him and the room in which he sat. Those images, electronically integrated and coded, were carried by a wide-band maser signal away from Luna at a speed just under 300,000 kilometers per second. Crossing from Luna to Earth took almost one and three-tenths seconds. It took that much more time for a returning signal to reach him from Earth. A little over two and one half seconds had passed, therefore, when the analogue image smiled and spoke. "Hello, Bob."

"Hello, Jarl."

Jarl Emmett, Operations Supervisor of STC Central, shifted in his chair, pulled a cigar from his coat pocket and puffed it alight.

"Have you heard, Bob?" Emmett asked, blowing a puff of smoke that billowed against the pseudo-wall that separated them.

"I've heard," Janas answered. While waiting for the signal to cross to Earth and its reply to come, he took a drink from the glass in his hand.

"Altho just couldn't wait," Emmett said angrily. "He didn't tell us anything before he did it. The first I heard of it was on a newscast less than an hour ago."

Janas nodded, but did not speak.

"Hell, Bob, I don't know how to react," Emmett said. "Maybe you can still talk to him, though I doubt it. He's committed himself, and I don't think he could back down now even if he wanted to."

"What about a board meeting?" Janas asked when Emmett paused. "He *is* an *elected* official."

"Elected, hell," Emmett snorted after the delay. "I'm sorry, Bob, but have you ever heard of a Franken being removed from the presidency?"

Janas shook his head slowly.

"And even if we thought we could we don't have that much strength on the board. Most of its members have been trying to get him to do this for months anyway."

"We can't give up now," Janas said coldly. "We've got to try everything possible."

Emmett looked around himself suddenly, as if fearful that someone might be listening in, though there would be no way of detecting a signal tap if there were anyone who wished to tap an analogue signal and had the proper equipment to do it—and both the Federation and Altho Franken had such equipment.

"You're right," Emmett said at last. "We'll talk about it when you get here. How soon does your ferry leave?"

Janas glanced at his wrist. "About an hour and a half."

"Okay," Emmett said after the light-speed delay had passed. "I'll meet you at the spaceport when you get there. Is there anything else?"

For a moment Janas was silent, then shook his head.

"Have a good trip, Bob," Emmett's image said as his hand moved toward the control console on his right.

Janas smiled back but did not speak.

The wall before him flickered and then returned to opacity, and for a long while Janas did not move.

At last, as if under a great weight, he lifted the glass to his mouth and downed the remainder of the Brajen whiskey. Savagely wiping his mouth with the back of his hand he rose, picked up his attaché case, and left the booth.

Chapter II

About seven and a half parsecs from Sol and her third planet, Earth, capital and founder of the Terran Federation, out in the direction of the constellation Aquila, far, far beyond bright Altair, lay a line of picket ships and unmanned scanners, each decorated with the "TF" of the Federation, alert for the enormous enemy fleet that reports said was now on its way toward ancient Earth, sweeping in from the worlds of the Rim.

One such picket ship, the TFSS *Douglas MacArthur*, lying in the void light-years from any star, tended one of its half dozen automated Non-space scanners. When the *MacArthur's* technicians had completed their check-out of the huge metallic globe, it was cast back into space and carried away from the *MacArthur* by chemical rockets. When the scanner, designated MAC-5, had moved some five hundred kilometers from its mother ship, it halted. For a long time it sat motionless as its energy banks accumulated power, while Jump Units inside it reached potential.

When a sufficient energy potential had been accumulated within the device a shimmering light grew up in space around it. To human eyes, had any been close enough to see it, space around the globe would have taken on an appearance similar to the shimmering of air above a heated pavement during a hot summer day on Earth. A force that simulated a tremendous gravitational field held in very close confines—though, of course, it was actually something radically different, but within the fabric of space-time that did not matter—grew up around the scanner; subtly at first, then with a stronger force, it began to warp the space around it, began to rip a hole in the very substance of the universe.

Then suddenly, the normal universe could no longer accept the presence of this thing that had no business being there, and violently spit out the globe. There was a tremendous energy discharge—not unlike lightning in a planet's atmosphere, though far greater than any lightning Earth had never seen—and the scanner was gone, was no longer within the space-time continuum.

To say that Non-space is "beside" the normal space-time universe is a weak analogy but better than none at all. Some had explained it this way: imagine two-dimensional universes stacked atop one another like sheets of paper, not quite, but almost touching; imagine further that the two-dimensional creatures, intelligences if you will, of one universe are unable to "see" the next universe beside theirs, though the actual three-dimensional space separation might be but centimeters; imagine now that *they* develop some means of passing across this space, of "jumping" through the intervening centimeters. Thus it was with mankind and his "three-dimensional" universe called "space-time" and that *other* continuum called, for want of a better name, Non-space.

And thus it was with the scanning device MAC-5 from the TF starship *Douglas MacArthur*. Spit violently from the three-dimensional macrocosm of mankind, it crossed the "four-(five) dimensional" space between and found itself in a second continuum.

The scanning device entered this suitcase cosmos, this matchbox universe that was, in size, a mere fraction of space-time. Non-space existed in its own right, independent of space-time, a complete universe, though lacking in the wealth of stars and dust that characterised space-time.

Imagine the two sheets of paper separated by centimeters. Imagine one sheet—call it "space-time"—as being large, and the other, "Non-space," as being on a much smaller scale, a tenth the size of "space-time," let us say. Now, pick a spot on the sheet called "space-time" and pick a corresponding spot on the sheet called "Non-space." Let us call them A and A^1. Now, pick another spot on "space time" and call it B and the corresponding spot, to scale, on "Non-space," B^1. The distance from A to B on "space-time" is, let us say, ten centimeters, but on the sheet called "Non-space," the scale of A^1 to B^1 is but one centimeter. Moving from A to B at a fixed rate of speed, for example, one centimeter per hour, would take, of course, ten hours—but at the same speed, we can move from A^1 to B^1 in only one hour—and yet the two sets of points are spatially equivalent!

This again is a weak analogy, but the idea is there. From Sol to Altair at the speed of light—a 5.06 year trip in space-time; in Non-space, light would take only a little over an hour and a half!

MAC-5 came to life, dozens of instruments began to scan the formless grayness of Non-space, while energy, not unlike St. Elmo's Fire, sparkled on the surface of the globe, dissipating into the hungry void of Non-space. The instruments ignored the dwindling sparkles and probed deeply into the expressways of the galaxy, searching for the approaching warships of General Henri Kantralas and the rebels of the Alliance of Independent Worlds which he led.

A scanner's minimum stay in Non-space was five hours, for it took that long for its Jump Units to reach sufficient potential to return to normal space and report to its mother ships what it had seen. That time had almost passed for MAC-5 when its laser-radar picked up something, detected movement far off in the grayness. Its computer analyzed the returning signal, found how much the signal had dopplered, determined the speed and distance of the approaching craft, then fed that information into memory banks. The laser-radar continued to scan, discovered other moving craft, and, sweep by sweep, determined something of the size of the approaching force. When the five hours had passed automatic relays closed in the Jump Unit, potentials became actual, and MAC-5 passed out of Non-space back into the black and starry universe where the starship *Douglas MacArthur* waited.

MAC-5 immediately established contact with the computer aboard its mother ship and, in the ultra-high-speed chatter of such machines, relayed the information it had gathered. Then, at a much slower pace, the *MacArthur*'s computer relayed that information to its human crew.

The captain of the *MacArthur* read out the information that came to him on a long ribbon of paper, printed out by the computer in terms that could easily be read by humans. The rebels were coming in force, the report said, though exactly how great that force MAC-5 had not determined. The enemy was at least as strong as the fleet that was on its way from

Earth, and perhaps stronger. In another hour MAC-6 would return from Non-space, if the rebels did not detect and destroy it, and would probably be able to give more detailed information. The *MacArthur*'s captain did not have time to wait; the information he had would be sent at once to the fleet coming from Earth.

Deep within the *MacArthur* a crew was standing ready with a portable Jump Unit and three message capsules. The captain gave the crew the message tapes to place within the capsules, and moments later the Jump Unit was rolled out through the air locks and cast into space. Rockets carried it as far from the starship as the scanner had gone, and it too passed out of normal space.

Once in Non-space the capsules released their hold on the Jump Unit and fired their plasma jets. With an acceleration that would have destroyed human flesh and bone, despite Contra-grav, the capsules moved away, spewing behind them stripped atoms that were quickly lost to the energy-hungry fabric of Non-space.

The three capsules were programed to search for the fleet that came from Earth and to inform them of the rebel's approach. The first to find the fleet would inform its fellows of its success, and the remaining capsules would drive toward their secondary goal, Earth itself, so that the Federation's capital might know.

Then the starship *Douglas MacArthur* waited, waited for MAC-6 to complete its scan of Non-space and return with further information, waited for the approaching enemy to discover the scanners and then enter normal space to find their source, waited for the enemy and death.

The captain of the *MacArthur* stood on the bridge, peering out at the vastness of space, and there was a cold sweat on his brow. His crew was ready. Energy cannon were manned. Missiles were primed. But he knew; he knew. That was the job of the pickets. They were not even the first line of defense; their only job was to look, to search, to find—and to be found. Then their job was done and they could die, but die fighting.

The captain of the *MacArthur* felt a chill down his back, but he did not show his fear to his crew.

Chapter III

The trip from Luna to Earth could be as short as five hours or as long as fifteen, depending on a number of factors. Janas and a handful of other passengers had elected to take the express ferry down to Flagstaff; it left an hour after the luxury boat but would reach the sprawling human habitations and spaceship facilities some six hours sooner.

The landscape below lay in darkness when the Luna-Earth ferry slipped into the terrestrial atmosphere and plummeted down toward the huge, sprawling complexes of southwest North America. Through the scuttling, moonlit clouds Janas could see the lights that marked the long ribbon city of Phoenix-Tucson, a string of glittering gems laid across the rugged countryside. To the north and slightly to the east of the cluster of lights that was Phoenix proper, was another, though dimmer sparkle. Dwarfed by the brilliance of Phoenix-Tucson, these lights were also those of a metropolis, the spaceport city of Flagstaff perched on the Colorado Plateau.

The ferry slowed its plunge, braked as it passed through a thin, high altitude layer of clouds, and was moving quite slowly when the lights of the spaceport broke apart into distinct spots of illumination. Moments later it touched the surface of the concrete and steel landing facility with all the velocity of a feather.

As light blinked on inside the ferry's main cabin Robert Janas unsnapped the belt that held his waist. He rose to his feet, picked up his attaché case and followed the other passengers out, through the con-tube and into the hoverbus that waited to take them to the terminal buildings some seven kilometers away.

Less than five minutes later Janas stepped out of the hoverbus and walked into the terminal, glancing anxiously around for the familiar face of Jarl Emmett. He was not there, at least not at the gate.

Janas had walked only a few meters into the crowded terminal when a boy, dressed in the uniform of a messenger service, hesitantly approached him.

"Are you Captain Robert Janas, sir?" the boy asked.

"Yes, I am," Janas told him.

"I have a message for you, sir," he said. "Please sign here."

Janas scrawled his signature across the pad, thumb-printed it, accepted the offered envelope, and dropped a tiny gold coin into the boy's waiting hand.

"Thank you, sir."

As the messenger boy turned and vanished into the

crowd Janas opened the envelope. Inside was a single slip of paper on which were written only two words: "Eddie's. Jarl."

Odd, Janas thought, but I suppose he has his reasons.

Taking an express slidewalk across the crowded terminal complex, Janas hailed a taxi. He hardly noticed the man who quietly, expressionlessly followed him.

*

Janas took the hovercab into downtown Flagstaff but decided to get out before he reached his destination. He had a sudden desire to walk in the night air, to see and hear the sights and sounds, for he was again on Earth after a long absence and wished a few moments alone on his home world before plunging into the problems that awaited him.

It was autumn in the northern hemisphere when Robert Janas returned to Earth, and there was a chill in the air despite the heat that rose from the city streets. His uniform had been designed for a warmer world than Earth, but he found the coolness pleasant after the artificial environment in which he had lived since leaving Odin. The air in the mountain city was clean and clear, for the city fathers of Flagstaff were strict and cautious about what impurities they allowed to escape into the atmosphere. The lights of the city hid the stars, masking them in their perpetual glow so that the whole sky seemed to be a leaden gray, though that did not bother Janas. Earth's night sky was one of her less spectacular beauties, especially after one had seen the night skies of Odin.

Even though the hour was late the streets of Flagstaff were filled with people, for Earth was a planet whose inhabitants had nearly forgotten the diurnal rotation of their home planet.

Little attention was paid to Janas' uniform: the blue and gold of an STC starship captain was not an uncommon sight in this spaceport city of the western hemisphere. Janas found the clothing of the inhabitants of Flagstaff far stranger than they found his.

During his absence from his home world the endless wheel of fashion had turned through half its cycle. When he last saw Earth—was it really a decade ago?—women had covered themselves demurely—high collars, long sleeves, long skirts, rather sober and conservative colors. Now all that was gone. Young girls in the streets of Flagstaff wore the briefest of costumes, ignoring the air's autumn chill. Brightly colored blouses, sometimes of shimmering, changing colors, sometimes all but transparent or consisting of no more than billowing sleeves and low-cut backs, showing supple, attractive young bodies, arrogantly exposing their firm breasts to the world. Skirts, as brightly colored, were frequently just long enough to justify their name. Necklaces of glittering beads and metallic disks, bracelets and anklets of shimmering plastics, threw back dancing sparkles of light, bright against pink flesh. Piled high above their heads they wore elaborate mountains of hair, often of colors never evolved by terrestrial mammals.

Men's clothing had undergone a similar change. No longer were the men of Earth satisfied with loosefitting, somber-colored jackets and trousers. Billowing, silken shirts and skin-tight pants, often decorated with brilliant stripes and patterns, here and there sporting elaborate fringes and lace, gave men the appearance of medieval jesters and harlequins, renaissance dandies. To Janas the most disconcerting aspect of the new masculine fashions were the grotesquely padded, clashingly colored codpieces worn by most of the men.

Janas did not approve of the present fashions, though he had seen more sensual and revealing costumes—or lack of them—on other worlds. But this is Earth, he thought. These are the people who set the trends for mankind, who establish humanity's concepts of taste. Still, he reminded himself, it's none of my business.

There were more changes in Flagstaff than the flashy, sensual costumes. The lights of the city were brighter and gaudier than he remembered them; Flagstaff had more the appearance of a spaceport city on Orpheus or Loki than one would have expected to find in the chief port city of the capital of the Federation. Cheap bars and taverns, lewd show clubs and ill-disguised houses of prostitution had sprung up where, ten years before, there had been unspectacular shops catering to the tourist trade. The streets were filled with a rougher sort of people than he remembered, swaggering braves and their painted girls, soldiers, mercenaries, now in mufti, brought from half a thousand worlds to defend the Federation. The laughter was too loud, the happiness too forced. There was, even here, a sense of despair, decay, even fear. What was happening Out There, light-year upon light-year away, was having its effect on Earth, just the beginning of its effect.

Flagstaff had changed and with it Earth, and Robert Janas, born within a thousand kilometers of that city, was a stranger there.

An uneasy sensation ruffled the short hair on the back of his neck. He stopped suddenly in the middle of the crowded street and looked behind him. He thought that he saw a man turn away quickly and appear to be looking into a shop window, but whether the man had actually been following him he could not know for sure.

Why would anyone want to follow me, he asked himself, and he knew the answer almost before the question was framed in his mind. His reason for coming to Earth was still as real as it had been; the goal had not changed though the methods of implementing it might be modified—and modified in what manner Janas did not yet know. Yes, he told himself, there *might* be a good reason for someone to be following.

He walked on and soon saw the lights of his destination.

Entering Eddie's, allegedly the oldest bar in Flagstaff, Janas immediately located the men's toilet and entered. Locking the door of the small cubicle behind him he quickly undressed. The man who had appeared to be following him gave him an uneasy feeling that he would not be able to dispel until he was certain of some facts.

Standing almost nude in the center of the small room Janas opened his attaché case, took out a small, pen-shaped object, and began to carefully explore his clothing, holding the object several centimeters from the cloth. When he came to the back of the uniform coat, just below the collar, the device emitted a barely audible "beep," and a red jeweled light in its tip began to glow. Peering closely at the folds of the cloth Janas saw the object of his search. A centimeter or so in diameter, fixed with two small barbs to hold it in place, it was a tiny radio transmitter. Janas pulled it from the coat, dropped it to the floor and, kneeling above it, carefully pounded it to dust with the heel of his shoe.

He continued his search, covering every square centimeter of his clothing and his attaché case, and only when he had finished was he satisfied that no more electronic "bugs" had been placed on him.

Who had placed the "bug" on his coat, or when, he did not know. It could have been on any one of a dozen occasions since his arrival on Luna or even since he reached Earth. He could only be sure that he would be more cautious in the future.

Relieved that he had not been imagining things he dressed and left the room.

Chapter IV

With an acceleration that would have produced a force of something over sixty G's had it not been for Contra-grav, the armada from Terra's moon reached approximately the orbit of Saturn. Orders had been given to the commanders of the starships, orders of Jump Sequence, orders of assembly in Nonspace, orders of battle when the rebels were met.

Some 1,419,000,000 kilometers from Sol, final Jump orders were issued by the flagship, the TFSS *Shilo*. Great shimmering fields of potential energy grew up around each starship, exactly matching the potential required to warp space sufficiently to force just that ship's mass out of normal space. The potential spheres flickered and shimmered and awaited the final command.

. Grand Admiral Abli Juliene himself gave that order, speaking into his throat mike as he sat strapped in a Jump seat on the flagship's bridge. At his command the potentials became actual, the fabric of the universe was twisted, transformed, burst, and the great mass of starships was spit like seeds out of the "real" continuum.

With the passing of an unbelievably sustained heartbeat the armada moved into a second universe, a grayness, a virtual nothingness.

The starships formed, regrouped and accelerated toward the spot where bright Altair stood in a coexistent universe, toward Altair and beyond.

The Terran Federation starship *Salamis*, heavy battle cruiser, was the fifth and mightiest to carry that name. She came from Earth, launched on her maiden voyage, moving toward the enemy fleet that menaced the heartland of the Federation. She led the fleet and behind her came the other battle cruisers and signal ships, their instruments scanning the grayness before them, searching to find, to engage, to destroy the enemy. The flagship of the mightiest armada ever put into space by the Federation, the heavy battle cruiser *Shilo*, followed in that pack, maintaining constant communications within the fleet.

Behind the battle cruisers came the destroyers, smaller, lighter craft, but no less deadly in their awesome weaponry. The destroyers swept through Non-space, spread out like an inverted cone, led by the famed *North Carolina*.

Following the cruisers and destroyers were the huge behemoths of space, the interceptor carriers, great spherical ships filled with small, fast, deadly interceptors. Out of Earth came the carriers, came the *Republic of Genoa* and the *Kingdom of France*, the *Commonwealth of South Asia* and the *United States of America*, and two dozen others named for the ancient states of Earth. Trailing behind the armada came the tenders and tugs, the repair and hospital ships, the great flotilla that kept a war fleet moving.

Outward went the armada, out to meet the enemy and determine the future of mankind.

Chapter V

Refusing to hand his attaché case over to the hat check girl, Janas quickly told the headwaiter that he was to meet Citizen Jarl Emmett there. That worthy smiled politely, bowed, and said, "Certainly, Captain Janas, Citizen Emmett is expecting you," and led him across the crowded floor to a dark corner where sat Jarl Emmett and three other men.

Off in the distance, moving among the tables, followed by a spot of illumination that seemed to have no place of origin other than herself, was a singer. She was wearing a bit of fog, sparkling as though diamonds hung within it. The mist clung to the rich contours of her body, not quite revealing but never actually concealing, either. Her greenish-white hair, as long as she was tall, climbed conically above her head, reached a peak perhaps half a meter high, then broke and spilled down across her shoulders, cascaded down her back, mingling with the mist that half-clothed her. A small, stringed instrument, something like a harp, was in her hands, and she plucked its strings as she walked. The song she sang was one that Janas had heard before, sometime, somewhere, long ago and far away.

> "We lie among the dwindling stars,
>   And Earth is far behind us;
> We jump across the universe,
>   But none will do us kindness;
> We ply the trades and wares of space,
>   And cry from pain and blindness.
> We have given you tomorrow,
>   And given up ourselves . . ."

Janas thought he recognized two of the three men with Emmett, though he could not remember their names at once. They looked up, smiled, and Emmett spoke.

"It's good to see you, Bob," he said, rising and extending his hand, "in the flesh, I mean."

Incongruously enough, Janas momentarily felt like laughing. There was something almost funny about the four darkly-clad men who sat around the small, oval table. Each had a partially empty glass before him and three were smoking. In the center of the table, virtually the only source of light in that corner, was an ancient, wax-encrusted wine bottle holding a burning candle. For an instant Janas was reminded of a scene from a 3-V production about bearded revolutionaries during the Crazy Years of the twentieth century, old style, but he did not laugh. Perhaps the analogy was too close for comfort.

Janas seated himself in the single empty chair, seeing, as he did so, out of the corner of his eye, the man whom he had suspected of following him on the street. He sat so that he could watch the stranger.

The smoke-clad singer had shifted to another song, a mysterious, free-verse thing with a melody that was not quite music to human ears:

"The grass was brown as winter wind could
        make it.
The trees were a blunt gray-green against
        the bitter sky.
The remains of a snowfall littered the
        earth's face,
And the air was a crisp, crackling cold
        when it stirred—
As the cold air stirred against his face and
        I listened,
And I heard the world whistle as it turned."

"You remember Hal Danser, don't you?" Emmett, who was dressed in a less gaudy edition of current terrestrial fashions, asked him.

"Hello, Hal," Janas said, shaking his hand across the table. "You're in operations too, aren't you?"

"I'm Jarl's assistant now," Danser said. "It's good to meet you again, sir." Slightly overweight, Danser's yellow and orange costume made Janas think of a huge, partially deflated beachball.

Janas turned to the short, thin man on his right.

"Juan Kai," the other said. "Operations Chief Engineer."

"I've heard a lot about you, Citizen Kai," Janas said.

Kai flashed a quick, toothy smile. "I hope it wasn't all bad, captain."

"Quite the contrary," Janas answered, then turned to greet the soberly clad man on his left. "Mr. Paul

D'Lugan, isn't it?" Even though he wore civilian clothes, there was a harsh, military cut to them.

A darkness crossed the face of the short, stocky, curly-haired young man. He nodded.

"You were first mate of the STCSS *City of Florence*," Janas said. "You brought two of her lifeboats back to Isis after the Battle of '77. You were something of a celebrity."

D'Lugan nodded again. "Not much heroism in that, captain. Federation ships claimed they mistook us for rebels. Cut us down before we had a chance to respond. Twenty-eight of us got out."

"I know," Janas said. "It was a terrible accident."

D'Lugan smiled coldly, seeming to question the accidental nature of the event, but did not speak.

The singer had vanished and now light began to glow at one end of the large room, gradually coming up to illuminate a low stage backed by a shimmering, golden curtain. When the white light had reached its maximum, casting a soft, shadowless radiance across the stage, a hidden band began to play a melody unknown to Janas. A small man dressed in a bright red and gold harlequin's costume pushed the curtains aside and stepped out onto the stage.

"Ladies and gentlemen," he said as a hush fell over the crowd, "Eddie's is proud to have with us tonight one of the most exciting dance teams in the known galaxy." He paused dramatically. "Straight from Odin itself—let's give them a big hand—Rinni and Gray, the Moondog Dancers."

After an appropriate amount of applause the golden curtains opened to reveal a crude imitation—to Janas, at least—of the rugged, starkly beautiful Odinese Craterlands. The backdrop of myriads of bright, glittering stars was a fair replica of Odin's night sky, all the brilliance of the Cluster. The hidden band played louder still, swinging into a much modified version of one of the traditional songs of the rebellious, unconventional Odinese Moondoggers.

A few moments later a troupe of a dozen nearly nude girls, wearing just enough to give an impression of the unorthodox costumes of the Moondoggers, danced out onto the stage and began an elaborate routine that had little to do with the planet Odin—now or ever.

Janas looked back at the men seated at the table. The three with Jarl Emmett were fellow "conspirators," and he distrusted them for it, as he unconsciously, unwillingly distrusted most of the men whom Emmett had recruited in his campaign to maintain STC neutrality, though Janas knew very few of them personally. Oh, of course, he told himself, I'm one of them too—I started it—but, dammit, I still can't trust them, not until I know their motives. There are always too many men running around, ready to join any kind of revolutionary movement, men who feel that they could do better if the old way were destroyed and a new one established—oh, how rarely they were right!

Jarl's an excellent judge of men, though, he told himself. There's a good chance that these fellows are not innate revolutionaries but men who coldly and rationally understand that this is the only way that we can hope for anything to survive.

Janas glanced again at the man who sat a few tables away and seemed to be observing them in only the most casual, impersonal way. Who, what did *he* represent?

Seeming to sense Janas' uneasiness, Emmett opened his coat and briefly showed him a small, rectangular box suspended by a leather band under his arm. Janas recognized the device, called a *noiser*, an electronic scrambler designed to disrupt listening equipment that the stranger, or anyone else, might have trained on the five men at the table. Janas nodded.

"What's this all about, Jarl," he asked after a waiter had taken his order and returned with a chilled glass of Brajen whiskey.

Emmett cleared his throat, looked around uncomfortably, then spoke: "Everything's changed, Bob," he said. "Now that Franken's committed the STC to the Federation without waiting for your reports we've got to decide what we're going to do. That's why I wanted you to come here. I wanted you to meet the top men in the 'Committee' so that we can try to make some preliminary plans." Emmett paused for a moment, took a sip from his own glass, then looked at the others.

"I'm still more or less the chairman of the 'Committee,' " he said, then looked at Danser on his right. "Hal's my assistant in this as well as just about everything else. He's also our chief liaison man between Operations and the other departments." He gestured toward Kai. "Juan's in charge of keeping track of what's going on in space. As of this afternoon he's responsible for knowing where *all* STC ships are, how quickly they can aid the Federation, and how quickly we can contact them if we can get a countermanding order to Franken's commitment."

"Then the orders *have* gone out?" Janas asked.

"A little while after I talked to you," Emmett told him. "I did everything I could to stop them or hold them up but it wasn't any use."

"Did you talk with Altho?" Janas asked.

Emmett shook his head. "I could only get as far as his personal secretary, a young snot named Milt Anchor. Anchor ran me around Robin Hood's barn and then gave me a story about Franken being in conference and would call me when he got finished."

"And he never called," Janas said, only half a question.

"Never," Emmett answered, shaking his head again.

"He won't, either," Paul D'Lugan said.

When Janas turned to face him the younger man returned his gaze, stare for stare.

"I'm head of the action department, captain, rough and tumble stuff," D'Lugan said in answer to Janas' unspoken question: "I'm the black sheep of the outfit. I'm not too popular with my friends here."

"That isn't so, Paul," Danser said quickly.

"Yes, it is," D'Lugan responded. "I'm advocating force, captain," he said to Janas. "If Franken won't listen to reason, and he's shown no indication of doing so thus far, I figure we're going to have to shove a gun in his belly and make him listen."

There was a moment of awkward silence. It was obvious to Janas that the others did not agree with D'Lugan, nor did he, not if he could help it.

Turning his head Janas glanced at the stage to see that a new couple had appeared and the twelve chorus girls had retreated to the background. He assumed that the newcomers, bathed in a cold, blue light, surrounded by dissipating mists, were the headliners of the show, Rinni and Gray, the Odinese Moondoggers. They *could* have been from Odin—or any other planet in the Spiral Arm—for they did not wear enough clothing to identify their place of origin.

Rinni was a tall, long-limbed blonde, graceful and very pretty in the exotic way of so many of the star worlds. Her long yellow-white hair swirled around her bare shoulders, across her naked breasts, billowed out behind her as she leaped and spun in a sensual dance with her partner. Gray was as handsome as Rinni was pretty—young, dark, muscular. Each wore nothing but a pale blue breechcloth decorated with a symbol in darker blue. Janas identified the sign as being something significant to the Moondog cult but could not remember its exact meaning.

Emmett's voice brought his attention back to the table.

"There's one more person I wanted you to meet," he was saying. "Syble Dian. She's our lawyer and head of our 'legal department,' if you want to call it that." Janas nodded. "She couldn't make it tonight," Emmett went on, "but she wants to meet you as soon as she can. She's something of an admirer of yours."

"Oh," Janas said, attempting a smile.

Emmett did not seem to hear his reply. His mind had gone on to something else, something that brought a dark scowl with it.

"An agent of the rebels contacted me this afternoon," he said at last.

"What did he want?" Janas asked.

"It was a *she*," Emmett said. "Called me on 3-V but had the visual blanked-out so I don't know what she looked like. Anyway, they have a 'cell' here in Flagstaff. She offered me their help."

"Help?" Janas wondered aloud.

"Offered to help us in whatever we decide to do," Emmett explained.

"What did you tell her?"

"Nothing."

"Good," Janas said. "We'd do better if we stayed clear of them. Their motives aren't the same as ours. We'll have enough problems without the 'help' of an outside group."

"That's what I figured," Emmett replied. "This is a family matter for the STC alone. We take care of our own." There was an almost sinister sound to his last words—and Paul D'Lugan smiled at them.

Emmett was silent for a moment, as if thinking carefully before he spoke again. "Bob," he said at last, "will you tell them exactly why you're here?" His gesture included the other three men at the table.

After taking a sip of his Brajen whiskey, Janas said: "I've brought two reports to show to Altho Franken. They're both on computer tapes, and typewritten. One is an analysis of the damage done to Federation worlds over the past decade or so."

"Don't you think that Chairman Herrera has informed him of the situation?" Hal Danser asked.

"No, not really," Janas said. "I doubt that Herrera told him any more than he was forced to if he really expected to get STC help, which he's gotten. I don't believe that Altho has any idea how bad things are out there or, at least, didn't know it when he agreed to let the Federation use STC ships and men."

"How bad is it?" Danser asked softly.

"Real damned bad!" D'Lugan snapped.

Janas glanced at D'Lugan. "Far worse for the Federation than they've been willing to admit. The rebels all but control the Rim. Federation forces always were spread too thin out there to really be effective. The Cluster's split wide open. The rebels certainly don't control it, but neither does the Federation. Right now the Cluster is fair game for anyone strong enough to hold it."

"What's left of it," D'Lugan added darkly.

Janas nodded. "The Cluster isn't the same place it was ten years ago. I hardly recognize it myself. Several planets that were inhabited aren't any longer."

"Antigone," D'Lugan said as if the word were almost sacred.

"That's one." Janas did not want to think of Antigone as he had last seen her, burning forests, seared plains, smoldering cities, all but wiped clean of life. "There are several others. I was on Odin for three years and I still find it hard to believe what's happened there. Earth and the Solar planets are the only ones that have escaped major destruction so far.

D'Lugan did not speak again but Janas saw a great depth of pain and sorrow in his eyes. He did not ask the younger man's reason for his grief. Danser sat quietly peering into the murkiness of his drink. Juan Kai fumbled another cigarette into his mouth while Emmett leaned forward across the table.

"The other report, Bob?"

"Okay," Janas answered, glancing down at the attaché case that sat on the floor beside him. Then he looked back at the others. "I won't even try to tell you how I got the information that I have or what it cost me. Just let me say that I'd stake my life on its accuracy."

"What is it?" Danser asked suddenly.

Janas glanced at the stranger who sat a few tables away. His left hand had gone to his ear and his face wore a puzzled expression. Janas smiled to himself and caught a similar smile in Emmett's eyes.

"A breakdown of General Kantralas' forces," Janas answered slowly, turning back to Danser. "A count of his men, his ships, his weapon strength. It's probably the most accurate information on the planet outside of Federation headquarters in Geneva.

"Part of this report is a 'psychological study' of Kantralas and each of his lieutenants," Janas went on. "I don't imagine it's any secret on Earth that Kantralas' force is held together by little more than the strength of his personality. There are just too many divergent forces, both personal and national, to make his army a really unified force. The only thing they have in common is a desire to beat the Federation."

"That's no secret," Emmett said. "Herrera's pushing it for all he's worth."

"Go on, captain," D'Lugan said, lighting his second cigarette.

Janas accepted a cigarette offered by Danser, sat back in his chair, took a sip of Brajen, and let his attention go briefly back to the lighted stage where the dance was rising toward a savage, sensual climax. He thought that Rinni and Gray had probably been to Odin at one time, or had at least studied the dances of the Moondoggers, for there was something in their motions that reminded him of Odin—but it was artificial, not quite genuine. They were good, Rinni and Gray; they made your pulse pound faster and caused a stirring inside you, but they were not Moondoggers—and in a strange way Janas was relieved that they were not. He turned back to his companions.

"They're following Kantralas," he said, "because he's the only man big enough to hold them together. They respect him and they know that no one of them alone could beat the Federation, and they think Kantralas can. Once he's done it, though, his power over them will be gone and they'll do as they please. Carman Dubourg plans to build his own little empire in the Outer Rim. Issac Holzman has the idea of cutting

Krishna off from the rest of mankind and making a
return to the old ways of his people. Half a dozen men
want to do as they please with the Cluster, but the
Cluster doesn't want any of them. And so on. There's
a lot of justice in some of their desires, but some of
the others are just plain naked power lust.

"Well, my report is a study of each of these men,
the ones who count, their personalities and motiva-
tions, and a projection of what they and their people
are likely to do if and when the Alliance has defeated
the Federation. If they win, despite the good inten-
tions of men like Kantralas and Holzman, this Spiral
Arm is due for a long period of internecine warfare
until one of them comes out on top or they've all
destroyed each other."

"That's exactly what Herrera's saying," D'Lugan said
coldly. "Are you agreeing with *him*?"

"No," Janas replied in the same tone of voice. "We
all know what kind of peace Herrera will give us. If
he can defeat the rebels and get his hands on the
STC there's nothing to stop him from doing anything
he wants. Herrera's a power mad dictator and the
kind of peace he'll give the Federation would be
worse than another hundred years of war."

Fighting down the feeling inside him Janas turned
to face away from D'Lugan, from the others at the
table, and refused to think of the terrible alternatives
facing mankind.

His eyes fell on the dancers on the stage and his
ears suddenly heard the rising beat of the drums, the
sensual screaming of the horns of the hidden band.
The dance was approaching its end, a startling, yet
inevitable climax.

Clasping each other savagely for a moment, Rinni
and Gray pushed themselves apart, stepped away,

and stood for a tense, pregnant moment peering into each other's eyes. Then, with a single movement, the girl and the young man ripped off their breechcloths, threw them away. The music screamed one final sensual scream, then stopped. There was total silence.

Rinni slowly sank to her knees on the carpeted stage, silhouetted against the starry backdrop, looking frankly and boldly at Gray, holding her arms out to him. As he crossed the two meter space between them and lowered himself to her the lights faded out and the stage vanished into the darkness.

"Either way mankind loses," Emmett was saying, darkly oblivious to the events on the stage. "There's a dark age coming, one that'll plunge this whole Spiral Arm into barbarism. Somebody's got to survive, somebody who can try to keep civilization going. And there's nobody who can do it but the Solar Trading Company."

"Jarl's right," Janas said. "And if you read these reports, you'll see that there's only one possible outcome, regardless of what the STC does. The Federation cannot possibly win this war. There'll be rebel forces on Earth within a month."

Chapter VI

The TFSS *Salamis*, leading the armada from Earth, now out past Altair, now over seven parsecs from Earth, made contact with one of the surviving picket ships, the TFSS *Pompey*, fleeing Earthward.

"The rebel fleet is near," the *Pompey* said in reply to a question from the armada. "God, is it big! We didn't know there were that many ships in the galaxy."

The *Salamis* acknowledged, told the picket ship to continue toward home, absorbed the information stored in its computer banks, and went forward, probing, scanning, peering into the grayness with electronic eyes, searching for the telltale emmissions of electronic and nuclear equipment.

The heavy battle cruisers formed up. Like a huge swarm of another continuum gnats, the cruisers grouped themselves in the center of the battle formation. Around them, making one vast encircling flank, were the destroyers. Behind this shield of metal and paraglas, of flesh and bone, ranged the carriers, their great ports open, tiny two-man interceptors ready to leap out into space once Abli Juliene, Grand Admiral of the Federation Expeditionary Force, gave his commands.

Those commands came. One after another two dozen interceptors burst from their mother ships, jetted forward ahead of the fleet at "max ack," and vanished into the grayness lying before the starships from Earth.

*

Despite the anti-acceleration forces of Contra-grav, Major Evan Branchi, pilot of the *Wanda Love*, commander of the TFEF "probe squadron," lay crushed against his acceleration cot as the tiny interceptor's plasma jets blasted into the grayness. Drugs circulating in his blood kept him awake despite the fierce acceleration that tried to steal consciousness from him. His eyes stayed open, peering at the screens and dials before him, watching the chronometer tick away the seconds.

Here we go, Branchi thought, and here they come. They can't be far away now.

The chronometer reached its cutoff point. A signal was sent through the interceptor, back to the plasma jets that threw it forward. The jets suddenly ceased their atomic flaming. The *Wanda Love* fell forward.

"Able Leader to Able Q," Branchi said into his throat mike. "This is it, gang. Radio silence from here on out—unless we're attacked. Otherwise, if you see anything, tell the fleet; don't talk to me."

There were brief acknowledgements from the twenty-three other ships, then the radio gear grew silent.

Branchi glanced over his shoulder to the young man who sat behind him.

"How is it, Jack?" he asked.

"Buttoned up tight, major," Jack answered. "We don't have a single leak that I can detect. The only emmission leaving *Wanda* is the tight beam back to *Shilo*."

Branchi nodded, turned back to his instruments, and watched and waited.

As the *Wanda Love* fell through Non-space she was little more than a derelict. Detection instruments outside her would hardly have known of her existence; drive cut off, scanning equipment reduced to a passive minimum, grav-control gear disabled, life support systems not operating. Her two man crew lived inside their spacesuits. Virtually the only electro-magnetic energy that escaped from the *Wanda Love* was a very tight radio beam aimed directly back toward the armada's flagship. Only by passing directly through the beam would the enemy be able to detect it.

Her job was to sweep in as close to the rebel fleet as possible, gather what information she could by passive detection gear, then turn back to rejoin the fleet. In the event of her discovery she would report what she had found to the fleet and then fight for her life. So it was with all twenty-four interceptors that fell toward the supposed location of the enemy.

The elapsed time chronometer continued to sweep its dial as the *Wanda Love* fell farther and farther away from the massive fleet from Earth. Evan Branchi felt an uneasiness in the pit of his stomach, that same sensation that he had felt on his first "probe" mission and had hoped would pass with time. It had not left him; never really left him even while secure behind the lines, or even on Earth herself, for Evan Branchi knew, as men are given to know few things, that one day, sooner or later, a "probe" mission would not turn out right, that one of them would go wrong, and Evan Branchi would never again see the green of Earth's hills, the blue of her sky.

This one may be it, he said to himself, as he had said a dozen times before on a dozen near-suicide missions. Before he had been wrong, wrong a dozen times—but this one made thirteen. Branchi was not a superstitious man, not in the Federation's tenth century, but still . . .

Passive detection gear operating on subtleties that would have gone unnoticed amid the electromagnetic storm of space-time sensed something ahead in the grayness, something unnatural, man-made, something that meant enemy interceptors!

"Do they see us?" Branchi's copilot asked, a tremor to his voice that betrayed his sudden fear.

"How can they miss us?" Branchi asked, the shakiness within him solidifying into something that passed for courage, into whatever it was that made him one of the best interceptor pilots in the fleet. "They have the same equipment we do." His voice was as calm and solid as the Rocky Mountains.

"What do we do?"

"Kill 'em," Branchi said through his teeth, his hands dropping to the controls before him. Active scanning gear came to life, sharply outlining the enemy craft on his screens: sixteen rebel interceptors, bearing on a course that would take them within a few kilometers of Branchi's path. Then the plasma jets fired; the radio broke silence.

"Able Leader to Able Q," he said. "Contacted rebel scouts." He read off a list of coordinates for the benefit of the armada behind them. "Orders are to engage and destroy."

The *Wanda Love*, suddenly a living thing beneath his hands, cut a wide arc through the grayness of Non-space and swung to make a lateral attack on the enemy that had also come to sudden life.

The two small interceptor squadrons were still hundreds of kilometers apart when they began to exchange fire. Energy cannon burst in the grayness, swinging through the space between ships. Sprays of electrical energy sparkled across metal hulls. Light flashed where there had been no light before.

For an instant Branchi wished that he were on a larger ship, one big enough to hold force screen generators . . .

The *Wanda Love* led the Federation interceptors in their rush toward death—and she was the first to feel the full force of the energy blasts of the enemy sweeping across her bow. Electric flame swept up across her needle-like shape, searing, then melting metal and paraglas. The *Wanda Love* exploded as a second fifth-level energy blast caught her hull—and Major Evan Branchi, TFSF, died as his spacesuit ruptured into the vacuum of Non-space.

Chapter VII

Janas thought that the morning was unexpectedly cool as he stood looking out of the window toward the park behind the house. A breeze ruffled the brown leaves of a small bush a few meters from the window, sending a sympathetic chill down his spine. A cold front had moved in during the night, heralding the coming chill of winter, and Janas found something prophetic in it, something that matched his own feelings and that seemed to foretell the coming catastrophe. He tried to shrug off the feeling but it would not go, and he quietly resigned himself to it.

There was a knock on the door behind him.

"Yes," he answered.

"Are you awake?" asked the voice of Miriam Lysek, Jarl Emmett's wife, through the wooden door.

"Sure," Janas answered. "Just a minute," he added as he took his robe from the chair beside the bed and slipped it on. Then he crossed to the door and opened it.

"Did you sleep well?" asked Miriam, a small, attractive woman, twenty or thirty years younger than her husband.

"Yes, but not long enough," he answered her.

"Stay in bed as long as you like," she said. "Jarl and

I have to go to work. Your breakfast's in the hotbox when you want it."

"Thanks. I think I'm about ready for it now."

"Jarl said to give him a call later on."

"I'll do that."

"Okay. See you later." And with that Miriam made her exit, leaving Janas again alone in the Emmett's guest room where he had spent the short night.

After taking his shaving equipment from one of his suitcases Janas went into the bathroom to shave and bathe, hoping that these would help to dispel the feeling of gloom that hung over him.

While he shaved, the steam of the bath swirling up around him, Janas thought about the night before. Jarl had flown him, Hal Danser, Juan Kai and Paul D'Lugan from Flagstaff to STC Central in a rented helicopter. During the flight the question had been asked again: "What do we do now?" Franken had violated his promise to Janas and had acted without the information that Janas carried in his attaché case. How could Franken's act be undone? How could STC support of the Federation be withdrawn?

Paul D'Lugan advocated violence—gather sufficient men and storm Franken's office by force, demanding that he withdraw his commitment to the Federation and call back the STC ships that now went to the Federation's aid. Janas had said, "No!" Franken was still his friend and had probably acted properly within the scope of his knowledge. Janas would go to him and show him the facts and request that he act in accordance with them. D'Lugan laughed bitterly. Franken could not and would not call back his orders willingly, he said. Janas, with the agreement of Jarl Emmett and Juan Kai, said that violence was too risky and uncertain—and at best should be used only as a last resort. Though he said this aloud Janas was strangely unwilling to admit to himself that violence might be the only course of action available to them. D'Lugan snorted but said that he would wait until Janas talked himself blue in the face, and *then* they would storm Franken's office and force him to save the STC.

Janas climbed into the hot bath, feeling the water rise over his thighs and buttocks, a warm, gentle caress. For a moment he thought of nothing, did nothing except relax and let the heat drain the tensions out of his body.

A few minutes later, clad in a fresh dress uniform, Janas went into the kitchen and took his breakfast out of the hotbox. As he sat down to eat he noticed a note on the table.

"Bob," the note said, "here are the keys to the yellow Holt in the garage. Use it as long as you like. Jarl."

Janas smiled as he dropped the keys to the hovercar into his pocket and then dug into his breakfast.

＊

It was the same as always, Janas thought as he drove the yellow hovercar out of the residential section of Central and down into the official districts.

Little had changed among the buildings and streets of the small city that made up the central offices of the Solar Trading Company. STC Central had grown gradually over a period of twelve hundred years, beginning at the place where the city of Prescott had once stood, and ten years had made little alteration in its appearance.

Standing starkly on the ancient Colorado Plateau, sheltered in a valley 1,980 meters above sea level, amid a land that had once harbored rough, wind-swept waste lands, side by side with vast grassy plains and dense pine forests, seared and burned bare by atomic fireballs before the days of the STC, Central had grown up slowly, proudly, as its starsips moved away from Earth, sought new, undamaged worlds among the stars. Now Central was old, a towering sequoia, its age not really hidden by fresh coats of paint, but it was still proud, still vigorous, still the home of the starships that ranged uncounted parsecs beyond the sky.

Janas went north into China Valley where the Academy still stood, seven hundred years in the same cluster of buildings, out to the place where young men trained as officers for the starships of the STC, and his mind slipped back to his own youth, so many decades ago, when he himself, full of hope, had trained there. He remembered those days well, too well, perhaps, and he remembered those who had trained there with him. Best of all he remembered the youngest son of Graham Franken, then president of the STC. Altho Franken, like Janas, had been fired with dreams of glory, but his dreams had gone be-yond those of young Robert Janas, who hoped for no more than the captaincy of a great interstellar liner. Al Franken, though he had three older brothers, aimed for the day when he would push past them and assume the presidency of the Solar Trading Com-pany. Our dreams came true, Janas told himself. Now what?

The borrowed hovercar sped past the low rambling buildings and across the wide fields where stood the fleets of training ships. He wheeled around and cut back south, toward the complex of Central, and toward the Altho Franken of now, the man who sat in the office of the president of the STC and made decisions that might well determine the future of mankind for the next thousand years.

Swinging the hovercar into a surface parking lot near the newest and most beautful building in STC Central, Janas parked, got out, and stood for a moment looking at the huge structure. It not only housed the office of the president of the STC, the largest and most powerful corporation in Man's portion of the galaxy, it was a monument to Altho's father, for this building had been the dream of Graham Franken's last years. Yet to Robert Janas, standing in the parking lot and admiring the structure, there was really something empty about its beauty. Perhaps, some part of his mind said, that is because it is not likely to be standing this time next year. It is not even likely to survive the winter.

A second hovercar pulled into the parking lot not far away. Its driver did not get out but sat still, apparently gazing off into space, though Janas had the distinct feeling that the stranger was peering at him.

Trying to ignore the despondency that filled him and his mild sense of apprehension, Janas left the parking lot and crossed to the Graham Franken building. The attaché case was cold and heavy in his hand and a sudden chill breeze ruffled his hair.

Inside the office building Janas crossed the magnificent main lobby with its tremendous mural, a pictorial history of the STC from the early days as Inner Planets Mining and Transportation Company to today when its ships traveled throughout the Federation and beyond. The other walls were decorated with the works of artists ranging from Botticelli to Wyeth, from Adamms to Senkowski. Hardly glancing either way, Janas crossed the lobby to the banks of escalators that rose from below the mural and climbed upwards into the building, disappearing behind the huge painting. On the fifth floor Janas changed from escalator to grav-elevator and rose to the uppermost point. Leaving the elevator he crossed the large room to the rows of receptionists.

"May I help you, captain?" asked the girl behind the desk he approached.

"I want to see Citizen Franken," Janas said simply.

"Which Citizen Franken, captain?" the girl asked, smiling pleasantly.

"Citizen Altho Franken."

"Do you have an appointment, captain?"

"No."

"May I ask your business with Citizen Franken, captain?"

"I'm Robert Janas. Citizen Franken will know my business."

"Citizen Franken is very busy," the girl said in a mechanical voice. "It is customary to have appointments well in advance. Could someone else help you?"

"No," Janas said flatly. "Tell him I'm here. I think he'll see me."

"Please have a seat and I'll call you, captain."

Janas smiled and went to sit down in a plush, overstuffed chair some few meters away.

The girl punched out a code on the communicator on her desk and in a few moments was speaking to some intermediary in the long chain between her and the man who ran the Solar Trading Company.

Though he could not hear the girl's words because of her hush hood, he could see the movement of her lips. Over the years as a commander of men Robert

Janas had picked up something of lip reading. He could at least follow the girl's end of the conversation.

"There is a Captain Robert Janas here to see Citizen Altho Franken," said the girl's moving lips. "No, he doesn't have an appointment. I don't know. He wouldn't say." Her lips did not move for a few moments. "Yes, ma'am, that's right. Captain Robert Janas." "Tall, dark, rather good looking in an odd sort of way." Janas smiled to himself. "Oh, I'm not sure. Maybe a hundred." "It is! Yes, ma'am."

The girl looked up at Janas and smiled, but did not speak. Janas smiled back and the girl bent to some papers on her desk, apparently passing him out of her mind.

Two more persons had approached her particular desk and requested to speak to someone in the STC hierarchy before the light of her communicator began to blink.

"Maura," the girl's lips said behind her hush hood as she flipped the communicator on. "Yes, ma'am," her lips said after a moment. "Yes, ma'am, I certainly will."

The girl rose and turned toward Janas. "Captain Janas," she said, "Citizen Franken will see you now. Please follow me."

Several people looked up in surprise at this stranger who was going in to see Citizen Altho Franken without an appointment weeks in advance. The name "Janas" passed across the lips of a few, and to some of them that name seemed to mean something.

The girl led Janas out of the reception room and down a long corridor. Twice she seemed about to speak but apparently thought better of it and remained silent. Janas was wondering why when they came to the desk of a dark young man, dressed in a conservative, old-fashioned business suit.

"Captain Robert Janas to see Citizen Franken," the girl said to the young man as he rose.

"Thank you, Maura. How do you do, captain," the young man said, offering his hand. "I am Milton Anchor, Citizen Franken's personal secretary. Citizen Franken is expecting you. Please go right in."

Janas thanked him, crossed the office and stood before the two huge, wooden doors, waiting until Anchor signaled Franken and then pressed a button that opened the doors.

Altho Franken, far across the huge, palatial office, rose to his feet.

"Bob," Franken said, "am I glad to see you!"

"It's good to see you again, Al," Janas said.

"Have a seat." Franken gestured toward a chair beside his big desk. "Care for a drink? Cigar?"

"No, thanks," Janas said, sitting down and taking a pack of cigarettes from his pocket.

"God, it's been a long time," Franken said, sitting back and pouring himself a drink from his desk bar.

Franken had aged, Janas thought. Ten years had added flesh to his body, creases to his face, grayness to his hair. His eyes seemed oddly recessed, almost hidden by dark, loose folds of flesh. There was a paleness about him that was more than lack of sun; it was a deeper, inward paleness such as prolonged fear gives to some people.

"How long has it been, Bob?" Franken asked.

"Ten years."

"It seems longer than that."

"It's been a busy ten years," Janas said.

"It has. A lot has happened, Bob, maybe more than

you realize. You haven't been on Earth. You don't know what's going on here."

"Maybe you don't know what's going on Out There," Janas said, gesturing toward the sky.

"You may be right," Franken said absently. He was silent for a few moments as he sipped the drink in his hand.

"How is Enid?" he asked at length.

Janas did not respond at once but looked at Franken, wondering how he knew about her.

"Oh, I keep tabs on my friends, Bob," Franken said with an overly friendly smile. "I know all about you and Enid."

Janas felt anger smoldering within him but fought it down. Al Franken had no business prying into his personal affairs—or did he?

"I'm sorry," Franken said in a conciliatory tone. "I mean, I had no intention of offending you. I just like to know what's going on."

Janas shrugged. Franken smiled and took a cigar from the ornate case on his desk. After wetting it he lit it with an old-fashioned lighter and leaned back in his chair. Janas let the incident pass, knowing that Franken was going on to an even more serious subject.

"Did I do the right thing, Bob?" he asked at last. There was something in his voice that told Janas that he did not want the truth but merely agreement. Janas could not do that.

"No," he said simply.

"I'm sorry you feel that way, Bob," he said, a slight sinking to his voice.

"It's not a feeling, Al," Janas said slowly. "I *know* you did the wrong thing."

"How can you know?" Franken asked suddenly.

"You haven't sat in this chair and watched the work of a thousand years begin to crumble around you. You *can't* know, Bob. You can't!"

"Do you know what's going on Out There, Al?"

"Of course I know," Franken said, almost in anger. "Every bit of available data was fed into one of the finest computers in the system. It came up with the conclusions, not me. I just acted on the facts."

"Have you been Out There? Have you seen what they've done to Odin? Do you know how badly off Isis is? Have you seen what's left of Antigone? Cassandra?"

"I haven't been out there," Franken said. "I couldn't go. There's too much to do here. But I have men out there. I have their reports and I've seen their tapes. I know what's going on Out There as well as you do, probably better."

"I doubt it."

"I have a thousand agents Out There, Bob. I receive reports almost every day."

"Spies, Al," Janas said. "And how do you know that their reports are true? How do you know that they aren't afraid to tell you the truth? How do you know they belong to you and not to the Federation?"

"Don't be melodramatic, Bob."

"I have my own reports, Al," Janas said. "It took me ten years, every cent I had and the lives of two of my friends to get them. You promised to read them before you committed yourself." He opened his attaché case. "Now submit these tapes to your computer and see what it says, then make up your mind."

"I've already made up my mind."

"I know," Janas said bitterly.

"I'm sorry, Bob. I wanted to wait until I had talked

with you but there wasn't time. I had to make my decision and I did. I'm sticking by it, Bob."

"Let me show you these reports!"

"I haven't the time," Franken said slowly. "I appreciate what you've done but it really doesn't matter now. I saw the Federation's reports and I have my own. You can't tell me anything I don't already know."

"For God's sake, Al . . ."

"Please, Bob, have a drink. I know it's been a rough ten years but you're home now."

Janas leaned back in his chair, savagely snuffing out a cigarette and reaching for another.

"Okay," he said slowly. "Give me a Brajen, Al."

"That's better," Franken said, smiling and reaching for the bottle.

"That doesn't mean I'm quitting, Al."

"I think you should. You're a Terran, Bob. I'd think you'd be arguing for me to *give* aid to the Federation."

"I'm not asking you to help the rebels."

"No?" Franken asked. "What do you want then?"

"I want you to keep the STC alive until this mess is over. I want the STC to live through what's coming."

"With our help the Federation stands a good chance of winning," Franken said, handing Janas his drink. "And besides, the Federation *is* the lawful government."

"Lawful government!" Janas said angrily. "Your ancestors never talked that way. The presidents in the old days never recognized any government's right to decide the life or death of the STC. They and the STC existed in their own right and knew that they didn't need anyone's approval to do it."

"Things have changed, Bob."

"They sure as hell have."

"Please, Bob." Franken paused. "We owe the Federation this much."

"We owe the Federation nothing, Al," Janas said, lifting the Brajen to his lips. "The STC built the first starships and opened up the stars. We made it possible for Earth to become united and to form the Federation with the planets *we* colonised. The STC made the Federation, Al. We owe the Federation nothing at all."

"You and I are citizens of the Federation," Franken said. "We owe it allegiance."

"Allegiance to a mockery? The Federation's a denial of the very principles that created it. It's an empire, Al, a sick, rotten empire. Henri Kantralas was a citizen too—is he the sort of man who avoids his responsibilities?"

"Kantralas is a rebel!"

"And Jonal Herrera is a tyrant," Janas replied. "He's a two-bit dictator who bribed and blackmailed his way to the chairmanship. He's dirt under your feet, Al. How can you deal with a man like that?"

"He *is* the Chairman," Franken said.

"Does that make everything he does right?"

"No," Franken said slowly, "but at least he has the law behind him."

"Law!" Janas snorted. "You always fall back on that. What does law mean to people like him? What does law mean to the Federation now? Do you think a man like Kantralas would involve himself with the rebel side if there were any justice in Herrera's cause?"

"Kantralas is a rebel," Franken said again. "He broke his oath to the Federation."

"He broke his oath, yes, and he did it in public, before the whole Federation. He hasn't kept anything a secret. Herrera breaks his oath of office a dozen times a day."

"I don't like Herrera either, but . . ."

"Why do you think Kantralas joined the rebels, Al?" Janas interrupted. "You don't know what the Federation's done Out There. They've left you and the STC alone because they weren't sure they could take on the STC while they were fighting the rebels, but that didn't stop them Out There. Why do you think the rebels have the popular support they have— and they *have* popular support, Al, despite what the Federation says. The people are fed up with the Federation and are willing to die rather than endure its tyranny any longer."

"I know they've had trouble Out There, Bob, but a lot of it couldn't be helped."

"And a hell of a lot more of it could have been!"

"What do you think I should have done?" Franken asked. "Thrown my support to Kantralas?"

"No," Janas answered. "Any open move to support the rebels would have brought the Federation down on you. Herrera wouldn't have wanted to open a second front, especially when things were going so badly in the Cluster, but he would have done it to keep you from helping the rebels.

"You should have kept out of it, Al, remained neutral. The STC has operated that way for twelve hundred years, and it should have stayed that way. The Federation wouldn't act against us as long as we didn't openly support the Alliance, and Kantralas would have recognized our neutrality."

"How do I know that?"

"You know what kind of man Kantralas is," Janas

said, "and you know that Herrera is afraid of the STC."

"Look, Bob, try to see it my way. If I had failed to support Herrera he would have held it against me. If the Federation wins Herrera would take the first opportunity to crush the STC."

"He'd do that anyway," Janas said. "But the Federation won't win. It can't."

"Wait," Franken said, an almost hysterical edge to his voice, "suppose Kantralas does win. He's an old man and there are a lot of younger men waiting to grab his power—and they *aren't* the kind of man he is. Kantralas will die or somebody will kill him, and then there's going to be hell to pay. One of those hotheads will try to take over the STC because he'll be afraid of us."

"Yes, I agree," Janas replied. "That's the point I'm trying to make. Look at the facts, Al. Read my reports. Once the Federation is beaten the Alliance of Independent Worlds won't hold together. There are a hundred and one systems just waiting for that moment to declare their *total* independence. The Alliance will fall apart within a year without a really strong personality—and a really strong reason—to hold it together. Then there won't be a single man or group strong enough to attack the STC and hope to win. We'll be the strongest power in the Spiral Arm."

"I still think our chances are better with the Federation."

"You wouldn't if you knew the facts."

"I know the facts, Bob."

"I don't think you do. Take Odin, for example. That's the most advanced planet in the Federation outside of Earth, or was. Odin has been building starships for centuries. It had the finest university in the Federation. It's ruins now, Al. The university is gone. The factories are destroyed. The spaceports have been all but smashed. Without help it will be five hundred years before Odin has the industrial facilities to build another starship. And Odin is better off than most. You don't build starships with the same industrial facilities you build steam engines, and the star worlds will be doing well to build steam engines when this is over.

"Someone's got to survive this war and the wars that will follow, Al. Someone who can help keep interstellar civilization going."

A strangely blank expression had come across Franken's face while Janas spoke. Finally he slowly rose from his desk saying, "I know you mean well, Bob, and I appreciate it. But I'm the one who has to make the decisions."

The door at the end of the large office opened and Franken's personal secretary, Milton Anchor, stepped in.

"Yes, Citizen Franken?"

"Captain Janas is leaving, Milt. Would you see that he has comfortable quarters? Nothing but the best." Turning to Janas he said, "Milt will read over your reports, Bob, and when he has given me a digest of them I'll talk with you again. Perhaps I can show you some Federation reports that will change your mind."

"I doubt it."

"You are planning on staying here in the hostel, aren't you?"

Janas shrugged, wondering where there was to go

now. Earth was no longer his home but he could not go back starward now, not yet, if ever.

"I'm staying," he said slowly.

Chapter VIII

The greatest armada of starships in Earth's history moved phantom-like through the grayness of Non-space, out to meet another fleet that might be larger still, and between them they would decide the fate of the thousand-year-old Terran Federation.

Nearly a millennium before, in the year 2504 by the old calendar, the city-states of Terra and the fledgling colonies of the star worlds, established by the great interstellar corporations that had dominated Terran political life for nearly two centuries, sent their representatives to the city of Geneva, South Central Europe, Earth. The Articles of Federation, drafted by that convention, bound all mankind into a single whole, a free and democratic republic. *Pax Terra* settled across Man's expanding domain, an era of peace during which the starships of the Solar Trading Company, older by nearly three centuries than the Federation and, in those days, more powerful, spread farther and farther into the stars, opening the Rim, colonizing the worlds of the Cluster.

The "Golden Age" of the Federation gradually became the "Imperium." Power and authority slowly gravitated to Geneva, into the hands of the Chairman, so subtly that few men even knew that it was taking place. As the centuries passed a sickness grew out of the dark places of the minds of the men who ruled the Federation, eating at the ancient freedoms of its citizens until, one after another, those freedoms existed only as privileges subject to revocation at any bureaucrat's despotic whim.

Eight hundred years after the Federation's founding the burden became too great, the sickness too vile. Here and there, on a dozen, then two dozen scattered worlds of the thousand ruled by the Federation, men began to gather together, to form grievance committees, to draft petitions, to demand redress.

In the beginning the Chairman could afford to ignore the isolated demands, could send in his hand-picked troops to quell disturbances and uprisings, but only for a while. Inexorably, beyond the control of any man, the idea of rebellion sprang from world to world. "Down with the Federation!" became a rallying cry, and the motto of the rebels became these words from an anonymous pamphlet: "Let us have done with old Earth; she has had her time. We shall offer up our lives, if need be, but somehow, someway, we shall strike out and make our own destinies."

The year 846 of the Federation was the year during which the worlds of the Rim, Orpheus, Loki, Prometheus, a dozen others, joined together and pledged themselves to bringing an end to the Federation. The Alliance of Independent Worlds was born.

Aware of the potential threat, the Chairman sent a fleet to crush the upstarts, warning others to stay clear of them or they too would feel the wrath of Federal indignation. The warships from Earth entered the Rim, bore down toward Orpheus—and met another, smaller, hastily assembled, poorly armed fleet. The rebels, what there were of them, had come to do battle.

The Alliance of Independent Worlds was very nearly destroyed during that battle. Decimated and scattered, their few remaining ships sought sanctuary. In Geneva the Chairman dismissed the Alliance from his mind; the threat was over, he thought.

Having learned the lesson well from their first encounter with the Federation, the rebels avoided open battle for the next seventy-five years. During that time, striking, raiding, plundering, recruiting and growing, the Alliance of Independent Worlds slowly and secretly swelled in power, becoming more and more prepared to again challenge the power of the Federation.

During this time the Solar Trading Company stood outside the politico-military arena, condemned by each side for trading with the other but too powerful for either to challenge. Formed during the age of the Terran city-states, the STC carried something of the ethos of a nation; those within it had come to consider themselves as citizens of no country save the STC. And the STC, ancient, fiercely proud, fiercely independent, fiercely dedicated to its own private goals, considered itself outside, if not above, *political* competition. Like the Switzerland of an earlier era, the STC followed its own course, oblivious of the varying opinions of mankind.

In the year 919 of the Federation Era, the Alliance took to the field again, confident of its newly gained strength, plunging its virgin fleets toward Earth, sweeping out of the Rim toward the capital of the Federation. The fleets of the TF confidently rose to meet them, sure of their superiority—but it was not so. The Federation fought the rebels to a standstill but could not gain a clear-cut victory.

Shocked by the rebel strength, perhaps even frightened, the Chairman and his advisors realized that mankind was due for a long, protracted war, one that would be waged all across the Spiral Arm, and prepared to meet the task.

Volumes could be written about this second stage of the Great Rebellion, as it came to be called, about the First and Second Battles of the Cluster, about the Skirmish of the Nebula, about the Meeting off Deneb, about the Defense of Rama: for seventy-five more years the Federation grew weaker and the Alliance grew stronger, and the day of final reckoning grew closer and closer.

Knowing that time was on the side of the enemy, the Chairman of the Federation, then Jonal Constantine Herrera, decided that nothing more could be wasted in indecisive battles, that no more offers could be made. The rebels *must* be driven back, destroyed, deprived of their will to fight. Wipe them from the universe, he told his commanders, use every means at hand; hesitate at nothing—this is no longer a gentleman's war!

And his commanders knew what he meant—rape, butcher, bomb cities and towns, devastate whole planets if necessary, but, in the name of the Federation, *win!*

One of his most gifted, most highly respected general officers refused to fight such a war of genocide and mass atrocity. Grand Admiral Henri Kantralas resigned from the Federation Space Force and was immediately placed under house arrest awaiting his trial for treason. Rescued by rebel sympathizers, spirited away to the the Rim. Kantralas became an anathema to the Federation and a rallying point for the Alliance.

Fired by a new hope, led by a man they had respected as an enemy and now idolized as an ally, the rebels prepared to meet the worst that Herrera could deal them—and did.

Sweeping into the Cluster and pouring down on Odin, citadel of learning and culture, Federation soldiers, led by the new Grand Admiral, Abli Juliene, placed the planet under martial law and began to exact their vengeance on its inhabitants. Women and girls were brutally raped in the streets of the cities of Odin; young men barbarically tortured to death for information they frequently did not possess; children butchered before their parents' eyes; fathers and mothers shot down in their homes for suspected disloyalty. Terror and madness settled over Odin.

Dozens of parsecs away Antigone, formerly neutral, was repelled by Federal brutality and declared for the Alliance. Again Federation ships swept in, brushing aside the feeble resistance that the rebels were able to mount in what time there was, and bathed Antigone in nuclear fire, leaving it a stark, blackened witness to Herrera's anger.

The rebels replied in kind, for the long, bitter war had reduced both sides to something less than human. Attacking and defeating the Federation stronghold on Cassandra, the rebel general Carman Dubourg returned rape for rape, murder for murder, atrocity for atrocity, finding new and still more horrible ways of maiming and killing the enemies of the Alliance. "Butcher" Dubourg gained his place in history, side by side with Attila the Hun and Adolf Hitler.

The Great Rebellion entered its third, most bloody,

and final phase, its first part marked by three great battles, and the greatest of these was the Third Battle of the Cluster.

Evenly matched, the fleets of the Federation and of the Alliance fought among the myriad bright stars— and none could say who won, for when it was over both sides retreated, swung back to their homes, the Federation ships to the Solar System, the rebels to the Rim, to lick their wounds and prepare for the next battle, one that both sides knew would be the greatest of all, and the last.

So it was when October came to Earth in 979 FE, when the thousand-year neutrality of the Solar Trading Company came to an end, when the great fleets moved to meet each other there in Non-space, some seven and a half parsecs from Earth.

Chapter IX

Janas accepted Franken's offer. If there were anywhere on Earth where he felt comfortable, it was in the Officer's Hostel of STC Central.

Following the fruitless conversation with Franken Janas allowed Milton Anchor to locate him quarters that were suitable to his rank and years of service. Finding himself satisfied with his suite, Janas returned the borrowed hovercar to the Emmett home, got his luggage together, and called a cab to take him back to the hostel.

Once established there he called Jarl Emmett and told him where he would be.

"I wish you hadn't done that, Bob," Emmett said.

"I don't want to be in your hair, Jarl," Janas told him.

"You're no bother," Emmett insisted. "Miriam wanted you to stay."

"I need some time alone, Jarl," he said. "And Miriam's got enough on her mind without an out-of-work starship captain under foot."

"Okay, have it your way," Emmett said with a smile. Then his face darkened seriously. "Did you talk with *him*?"

"Yes," Janas replied. "You were right. He won't listen."

"Do you have any other ideas?"

"No, not yet."

Emmett was silent for a moment.

"Look," he said at last, "I'll try to get together as many of the people as I can. Come over to my place about twenty tomorrow night."

Janas agreed to be there and broke the connection.

For a few moments he sat looking out the bedroom window, feeling something akin to indecision. Through the thin, now unpolarized sheet of paraglas, Janas could see a portion of STC Central spread out below him, a fantastic yet somehow beautiful collection of buildings of virtually every architectural style of the past twelve hundred years, in itself a history of the STC for anyone who wanted to take the time to examine it. Mount Union towered almost directly south, its peak rising something over two thousand meters into the clear, southwestern sky. Even now, fourteen hundred years later, its peak was smooth and rounded, almost glass-like. It had stood several hundred meters higher before the bomb hit it, before the thermonuclear fireball, one of several intended for Phoenix, rested for its instant of life, burning off the top of Mount Union and showering the valleys below with atomic hell. They said that there were still spots up there that would make a Geiger counter run wild, but Janas had never checked it out himself.

Turning away from the window, briefly hoping that there would never be another ball of fire rolling down the mountain slopes, hoping that the rebels would not find it necessary to bomb Central, Janas looked at the 3-V unit beside the bed. His indecision ended.

He punched the 3-V's Information key, waited a moment while Information clicked into the line, punched out the "Frisco Info" code. When it came in, Janas punched "C" and adjusted for medium scan. The names, address and call numbers of people in the San Francisco-Oakland Complex whose names began with "C" started to roll past within the tank; in a few moments the name "Campbell" had appeared and Janas slowed the rate of scan. When the name "Enid Campbell" came up he stopped the scan and began to write down a list of numbers. Cutting out Information, he punched the code number and waited.

A very attractive face, framed in auburn hair, appeared in the tank, the word "recording" superimposed over it.

"I'm out right now," the girl said, a pleasant smile on her face. "If you'll leave your number I'll call you back as soon as I get home."

"Record," Janas said into the unit. "Enid, this is Bob. I got to Flagstaff last night but this is the first chance I've had to call. Give me a buzz when you can. My code is FLC-21-77015-35. Stop."

A light flashed within the tank, indicating that the message had been recorded. Janas smiled and broke the connection.

After having a quick, solitary lunch in the hostel's canteen, Janas returned to his suite, ordered a chilled bottle of overly expensive Clytesian wine, and undressed. Before going to his bed to grab a few minutes of much needed sleep, he took the pen-like detector from his attaché case and carefully went over the clothing he had been wearing. He was not very surprised when he found another bead-like transmitter clinging to the cloth of his pants.

Snatching the "bug" from the fabric, Janas went into the bathroom and dropped the object into the toilet. As he flushed it, he thought with a smile; now let them figure out how I managed to go down the drain.

Once satisfied that no other "bugs" had been planted on his garments he lay back on the bed and lit a cigarette. Gazing at the ceiling, taking an occasional sip of wine, he had nearly fallen asleep when the 3-V unit beside his bed chimed.

Rolling over, almost spilling the wine, Janas punched the receiver button.

"Bob," a sparkling, feminine voice said before Janas was able to get into position to see the unit's tank, "are you there?"

"Yep," Janas said, finally sitting up and turning the 3-V toward the bed.

"In bed?" the girl asked. She was just as pretty as her recording. "This time of day?"

"Alone, too," Janas said smiling. "I didn't get much sleep last night."

"When did you get in?"

"I don't know, Enid," Janas said. "It must have

been around midnight when the ferry landed." He was silent for a moment. "You busy tonight?"

"No, of course not. I've been waiting for you. It seems like ages since I last saw you on Odin."

"It has been," Janas told her with a smile. "At least a million years. Look," he went on suddenly, "I'll rent a grav-car and buzz over this afternoon."

"You said you were tired."

"Not *that* tired."

"You know I want to see you, Bob," Enid said softly.

"I'll pick you up around seventeen o'clock," Janas said. "I have your address."

"I'll be ready."

" 'Bye," Janas said as he reached for the disconnect button.

Enid blew him a kiss as her image faded from the tank.

Downing the remainder of the Clytesian wine in his glass Janas rose, took a clean uniform out of one of his suitcases, shook the wrinkles out, and began to dress.

A few minutes later he called the hostel's main desk and ordered a grav-car, telling the clerk that he would be using it for about twenty-four hours. Before leaving the suite he dropped a small signal disrupting device that he had borrowed from Emmet into his pocket. He assumed that the grav-car would be "bugged" and he certainly had no intention of allowing anyone to listen to, or record, what was said and done between him and Enid. *That* was none of their business!

When he ascended to the roof deck an attendant pointed out a sparkling blue teardrop of steel and paraglas. The grav-car, its generators already running, hung quietly a few centimeters from the deck. A beautiful, luxurious and totally impractical means of conveyance, Janas told himself.

He tipped the attendant, climbed into the grav-car and lifted from the roof-deck of the STC Officer's Hostel. The buildings of Central shrunk below him, soon merging with the rugged countryside. As he climbed he could see the outlines of Flagstaff on his right and slightly to his rear. Behind him on his left was the huge, sprawling complex that marked the western terminus of the Phoenix-Tucson ribbon city, the vast conglomeration of buildings of Phoenix proper. Taking a last look at the scenery below he headed the craft northwest, across Skull Valley and toward the western coast that lay beyond the curve of the planet.

Under him Janas caught a brief glimpse of light reflected from the rotors of a helicopter headed west, apparently coming from the east of STC Central. During the flight he kept looking, thinking he would catch another glimpse of the craft, but he did not. Nevertheless Janas had the feeling that it was there, with him all the way to Frisco.

Leveling the craft off at about fifteen thousand meters, Janas pushed it up toward its top speed, adjusted the auto-control to agree with his flight plan, and sat back to relax. Traveling at slightly over four hundred kilometers per hour, Janas anticipated reaching the San Francisco-Oakland Complex in just a little more than two hours. In the meantime he planned to do very little other than look at the scenery below and remember the times he had spent with Enid on Odin.

When Janas had arrived on Odin, shortly after the Third Battle of the Cluster, the bulk of the Federation forces had withdrawn from that planet, leaving only enough men behind to keep the distraught populace in check. Falling back toward Earth, the Federation had regrouped and prepared for the final assault, which was then still three years away. The rebels, like the Federation, not yet ready to be drawn into another major battle, pulled back from the Cluster, leaving behind them a political near-vacuum. A shaky peace settled over the planet, frequently broken by bloody riots, cruel lynchings, ambushes and uncounted atrocities. The soldiers of the Federation retreated into the protection of the cities, while the thin veneer of civilization crumbled under the rising tide of anarchy. This was the world into which Janas stepped after turning his ship, the STCSS *President Regan*, over to his first mate—the ruined hell of a once beautiful planet. There was, at least, one pleasant aspect to it all.

Enid Campbell was the daughter of an official in the Federation Postal Service in University, the mail center for Odin. Ralph Campbell was in charge of incoming and outgoing extraplanetary mail, and in that capacity became acquainted with Janas, then Acting Manager of the Odin Major Terminal, and invited him into his home.

Campbell, Janas remembered with a still vivid pain, had died in the street fighting in University during one of the many riots; a funny little man who made a foolishly heroic stand to guard the mails against both the soldiers of the Federation and the Odinese nationalists. No one knew which side killed him, perhaps it did not really matter. Campbell had died doing what he believed to be right, and those who had killed him had probably been acting under the same belief.

Campbell had two children whom he had raised from near infancy after his term-wife's tragic, improbable death in a hovercar accident. The elder child was Enid, a startlingly pretty girl who had been born on Earth but had grown to womanhood on Odin of the Cluster. Her brother, Rod, was two years her junior, an idealistic and quick-tempered young man. Rod had left Odin, where he had been born and raised, a year and a half prior to his father's death. There were dark, secret purposes in Rod's journey to Earth that Enid only half understood. In his only letter to Enid, Rod had told her that he was living in the Frisco Complex from which the Campbell family had originally come.

As for Enid herself, Janas had found an immediate attractiveness in her, a girl young enough to be his grandchild or great grandchild in this age of two-hundred-year life spans. Yet they had bridged the gulf between them, Janas and this bright-eyed, wise-for-her-age girl, and they had become lovers. Janas had thought often of contracting marriage with her but had always fallen back on the same reason—excuse?—that had prevented him from marrying before: a starship captain has no business with a wife. He had not taken out a contract—but he had never entirely dismissed the idea.

For a brief span Janas relived his youth with Enid, starlit nights and laughter, but fate had other plans for him. There was a report forming in his desk, thousands of scraps of information that could help determine the future. And, too, the *darkness* was coming.

When conditions on Odin reached the point of almost total collapse Janas ordered Enid to return to Earth, to join her brother Rod in San Francisco, which was about as safe a place as there was in the Spiral Arm. Enid had argued, but she finally consented when Janas told her that he would also be returning to Earth soon.

The grav-car passed over the lower extremity of Lake Mede, afternoon sunlight sparkling on the expanse of water backed up by the huge, new Jonal Herrera Dam. Soon he crossed the orchards of Death Valley, and the San Francisco-Oakland Complex came into view.

The Frisco Traffic Control Computer broke into his reverie, asked his flight plan number. Janas' computer replied, and was soon given instructions for coming out of high altitude flight down into normal traffic patterns. Minutes later, dropping to a fourth of his former speed, Janas was in the chopper lanes a few hundred meters above the building tops. Shortly he came down into the surface lanes and, manually guiding the grav-car like a hovercraft, he followed the traffic flow into the part of the city in which Enid had taken up residence.

Strangely enough Enid was waiting outside her apartment building for him. The chill of the morning had passed and the afternoon had brought a breath of spring-like air into the city, a forlorn, poignant attempt to hold off the coming of winter. Enid Campbell had dressed for the moment of Indian Summer that filled the megalopolis that sprawled along the Pacific coast.

When she jumped up from the bench where she had been sitting, Janas saw that Enid had made concessions to the current terrestrial fashions. She wore a sparklingly iridescent frontless blouse, the shimmering, translucent cloth that covered her arms, shoulders and, he assumed, her back, dancing through a spectrum of colors as she moved. Her high, firm breasts jutted defiantly from between long, decorative lapels and high, arched collar. Her skirt, of the same material as the blouse, came almost to her knees, but its translucence left little of the shape of her hips and thighs to the imagination. Low cut white boots and a tiny cap of the same color completed her costume. All in all Janas found himself pleased but somewhat jealous—he did not want other men to see that much of her.

Swinging in toward the curb Janas brought the grav-car to a stop less than a meter from the spot where she stood. He leaped out and swept her into his arms.

"Bob!" Enid gasped after half fighting away from his hungry kiss. "Not out here."

"Get into the car then."

"Yes, master," she answered, and climbed into the vehicle while he held the door open. Janas entered behind her, seated himself, and in a moment the grav-car was moving again.

"Where to?" he asked.

"Anywhere."

"Supper?"

"Okay."

"Know of a good place?"

"Gaposchkin's."

"Where is it?"

While Enid directed Janas piloted the grav-car through the streets toward the restaurant.

"You seem to know your way around," Janas said a few minutes later, thoroughly lost in the maze of streets.

"I've had nothing to do for the past few weeks but study the city," Enid answered. "It's surprising how much you can learn in that short a time if you really put yourself to it."

"Found a job yet?"

"Not really. Haven't been looking. Waiting for you to come." She gave him a pixyish look and said, "I thought you might keep me off the streets and try to make an honest woman of me."

Before Janas could think of a good reply he found himself at the restaurant that Enid had suggested.

During the meal they talked the pointless yet significant, the almost-but-not-quite-nonsense talk of lovers who have been separated. It was not until they sat back, refusing dessert but ordering coffee, that the matter that had been hanging over them like an impending storm was brought up. It could not be avoided, not something that huge, that significant.

"Have you seen Altho Franken, Bob?" Enid asked, accepting Janas' offered cigarette.

Janas nodded.

"What did he say?"

"About what I expected him to say once I knew what he'd done," Janas said slowly. "He's committed the STC and he's not going to back down."

"What are you going to do?"

"I don't know yet."

They were silent for a few moments. A tiny, plump waitress, dressed in a too-revealing costume for her figure, brought their coffee.

Enid sat looking into the steaming cup of blackness for a while, as if seeing in the liquid some terrible vision of the future.

"Rod's going to kill him, Bob," she said at last, her voice weak and hollow, like a distant and all but forgotten echo.

"Altho?" Janas asked suddenly.

"No," Enid said, looking up from her coffee. "Herrera."

"The Chairman?"

"Yes. That's why he came to Earth. He's joined some organization—I'm not sure of their name—Sons of Liberty or something adolescent like that. But, Bob, they plan to assassinate Herrera."

"Your brother's an idiot."

"I know," the girl answered slowly. "He volunteered to do the shooting himself."

"What does he hope to accomplish?"

"I don't know," Enid answered weakly. "I don't even know if he knows."

"It's stupid," Janas told her. "That won't accomplish a thing. Kill Herrera and there'll be two more worse than he is ready to take his place. Does Rod have any idea how many times in history men have killed tyrants and discovered that they've made martyrs out of them and dictatorship that much more certain? Hasn't he ever heard of Julius Caesar—and does he know what became of Rome after *his* assassination?"

"I've told him that but he won't listen."

"If it were a well organized coup, something ready to wipe out all the underlings who support Herrera and take the Federation into strong hands, well, then it might be different. But just a harebrained scheme to kill him—that can't accomplish anything."

Enid sighed but did not speak.

"When do they plan to act?" Janas asked.

"I don't know," Enid said. "Soon, but I don't know when."

"We probably don't need to worry," Janas said, feeling a hard, cruel smile play across his face. "They'll probably never pull it off. In a few days, a few weeks, it won't matter much anyway—Herrera will be dead or far out of Rod's reach."

"What do you mean?"

"The Federation's not going to last much longer. I'm not sure, but I think the rebels are closing in for the kill now. Their fleet is massed and headed for Earth. There wasn't a single rebel warship in the Cluster when I left, and most of the Federation fleet left Luna yesterday."

"I didn't know it was going to be that soon," Enid said slowly. "I mean, it's been going on for so long now. I didn't expect it to end this suddenly."

"It won't end suddenly, darling," Janas told her softly. "It started long before I was born, and that was a long time ago, and the end of it won't come until long after I'm dead."

"But the Rebellion."

"The Rebellion will end soon, with a rebel victory. I'm sure of that. It's what's coming after that scares me."

Enid seemed to sense something of the fear that Janas expressed; it reflected in the deep pools of her eyes, mirrored in the hard tightening of her lips.

"I don't want to talk about it any more, Bob."

"I don't either," Janas said, rising and opening his wallet to pay the check. He dropped half a dozen golden STC coins on the table. "Where can we get a drink?"

An hour and a half and four Brajens apiece later, Janas and Enid returned to the grav-car parked outside the small, plush, dimly lit bar.

"Where to now?" Janas asked as they seated themselves.

"I don't know, Bob," Enid said, snuggling close to him as he revved the car's generator. "Anywhere."

"Your apartment?"

"No," she answered suddenly. "Oh, it's not that, Bob. I mean—" She smiled. "—it's just that I don't want to go *there*. I don't like it there. Rod is in the same building, him and his friends, and I don't want to see *them*."

"We could leave the lights off," Janas suggested jokingly, then realized how serious Enid was. "How about a cruise out over the Pacific?"

"That sounds lovely."

Janas contacted the traffic control computer and obtained a flight plan to take them up, out of the Frisco Complex and its strict traffic patterns. Five minutes later the super-city was a dwindling mass of lights below and behind them. Before them the dark, glittering ocean reflected a fragment of moon. The lights of one of the undersea settlements on the edge of the Continental Shelf glimmered through the water.

"It *is* pretty up here," Enid said. "So far away from everything. None of it seems real now."

"It's almost like being in space," Janas said, his voice sounding far away even to himself.

Below them a huge floating city slowly drifted past.

"Which one is that?" Enid asked, looking down.

"I don't know."

"Maybe it's *Atlantis*," she said. "I heard that it was coming toward Frisco this week."

"Probably is."

Enid slowly turned her head, her face heavily shadowed in the dim light from the grav-car's control panel. The look on her face showed that she knew that the time for talking had passed. Words were no longer necessary between them.

Janas' lips formed the words "I love you." Enid's

eyes replied and she pressed herself closer to him, slipping out of her almost nonexistent blouse even as she did so. As Janas reached for her, she began working with the buttons of his shirt.

*

The sun was rising above the Pacific when the grav-car returned to the San Francisco-Oakland Complex.

Enid had just finished dressing when they entered the surface traffic patterns. Janas smiled and told her that he couldn't understand the need to put her clothes back on; she was just about as naked with them as without. Enid gave him a sidelong glance of feminine wisdom and adjusted her skirt.

"How much money do you have?" he asked.

"I don't take money from men I like," Enid said, looking slyly from beneath her auburn curls. "My rates are pretty steep for fat old men, though."

"I mean it," Janas said seriously.

"Enough."

"Enough to move into a new apartment?"

"I suppose so, but why? I have a year's lease on the one I've got, paid up. It's good enough."

"No, its not."

"Why?"

"They know where you live."

"Who's *they?*"

"I'm not sure. Federation men. Altho's agents. Somebody following me. You're caught between me and your brother, Enid, and either one of us could bring you trouble. I've been followed ever since I got back to Earth. I don't want them, whoever they are, to be able to get their hands on you. Maybe I shouldn't have come out here to Frisco at all, but Altho knew you were here."

"What should I do?" Enid asked, the shadowy fear of the evening before coming back to her face.

"Hang around your apartment for a few hours," he told her. "Behave normally. Then take what you can carry with you without looking too conspicuous, make sure you're not being followed, and then find another apartment. Register under a false name. Don't tell me where you're going. It's better if I don't know."

"But, Bob . . ."

"Don't try to contact me for a few days," he answered sternly. "Wait until you know it's safe."

"How will I know?"

"I'll find some way of letting you know."

"I don't understand all this, Bob."

"It's just as well if you don't," Janas said. "But please, do as I say."

"Okay."

Janas brought the grav-car to a stop near her apartment. After a lingering kiss Enid climbed out of the car, an expression akin to pain on her face.

Looking back at her once, Janas pulled the car away from the curb and entered the traffic patterns. He did not look back again. He was afraid that he could not leave her if he did.

Chapter X

The enemy had begun to resolve on the scopes and screens of the warships of the Federation armada, and he was huge, far larger than anyone had expected. And it was muttered again, "We didn't know that there were that many ships in the galaxy."

It was an odd, a strange, a motley fleet, that of the Alliance, composed of Federation warships taken over by the rebels, of merchant ships converted for warfare, of ships they had built themselves before Federation warships had found and destroyed their factories. It was a strange fleet, but it was huge and it was blooded, a battle-hardened armada. They had held off the Federation for decades as they grew, and nów they had come again to fight, to take the war to the Federation's home, to throw all their forces into one last battle to determine the future of mankind.

The *Salamis* moved forward and the armada moved with her. The Federation had sent her ships on the same mission—settle it now; have done with it.

Very near the center of the Federation battle formation was the fleet's nerve center, the flagship, the TFSS *Shilo*. And on the bridge of the *Shilo*, sitting in the command seat, surrounded by his aides both human and electronic, was the man who was responsible for the fleet, Grand Admiral of the Federation Expeditionary Force, Abli Juliene.

The wait was intolerable. Though his eyes and ears were flooded with incoming data Admiral Juliene felt strangely apart, isolated from the events surrounding him, and he knew, deep inside him he knew, that the fate of the battle really did not rest in *his* hands but in the hands of another, a man who had once been his friend and superior officer—Commander-in-Chief of the Military Forces of the Alliance of Independent Worlds, General Henri Kantralas.

In his mind's eye Juliene could see Kantralas now, a little older perhaps, a little wiser, but still a huge hulking bear of a man, full bearded and monolithic, a childhood vision of the Jehovah of the *Old Testament*. That was the man he had come to fight, to destroy if he could, this man who had taught him most of what he knew of the arts of war, this man who was never at a loss, who was always confident, always right. Juliene shifted uneasily in his seat, feeling so small, so tired, so insignificant, and wondered how *he* could challenge such a man as Henri Kantralas.

But he did.

The first shot of the battle that would be remembered as long as men survived to remember it was delivered by the *Salamis*. Her great firing tubes slid open and vomited into the grayness of Non-space half a hundred nuclear tipped missiles. Force screens came up, enfolding the ships of both fleets in shimmering cocoons of energy. They met.

In that gray formlessness, lit by no stars such as Man's continuum is, the two colossi came together, warring with flame and lightning the likes of which the primeval gods could never have imagined. Forces that would have reduced a dozen Earths to smoldering cinders flickered and flashed, blasted and beamed between the ships. Ragnarok and Armageddon had come together, at one time, at one place. Limbo was filled with fury.

More than one rebel ship had died because of the *Salamis* when a barrage of energy cannon beams ripped open her shield of force. Nuclear missiles found their way toward the huge battle cruiser, but were met by energy cannon and exploded harmlessly still tens of kilometers from their destinations. The

Salamis struck back, her own cannon and missiles returning the fire of the enemy. Another rebel starship vanished in atomic flame, though moments later first-level energy cannon blasts of her companions reached the naked hull of the *Salamis*.

A direct energy beam ripped across her bow, searing into the thick hull plating, boring through into the ship—great gouts of white air puffed into space as if from a broken steam line. Liquid, glowing metal splattered outward. While sheets of electric fire shimmered across the starship's hull, the incoming blast reached her nerve center, her bridge. Bulkheads buckled; decks vanished in vapor; bank after bank of equipment ceased to exist. The captain of the *Salamis* and his bridge officers died.

Salamis fought on, commanded now from her auxiliary bridge, striking out in fury like a wounded animal. As her force screen returned she plunged still deeper into the heart of the motley rebel fleet, filling space around her with energy blasts and missiles, tearing into those who had come to menace the Earth that had made her. Other Federation ships followed her spearhead drive.

An enemy missile exploded in space during an instant when her screens were down to allow her own weapons to fire back. The nuclear explosion was some distance from the *Salamis*, but close enough to open her hull in another place, to send more of her precious air into the vacuum, to destroy the rest of the men who commanded her. The handful of surviving officers manning her auxiliary bridge died as heat and flame exploded around them, died holding fast to their controls, died returning the fury of the enemy.

For a moment the *Salamis* was like a dead thing, an empty, floating hulk to be destroyed or captured as the enemy saw fit. But that did not endure for long. The designers of the *Salamis* had done their work well; she did not die easily.

Deep within the starship's hull her master computer still functioned. The computer, in its quiet, mechanical way, tried alternate channels, called the command stations and received no answers. Relays clicked; tapes spun; electrons raced through circuit modules. The computer paused for a nanosecond, "read" its orders, then switched to "free-will" self-programming. The *Salamis* was still alive, perhaps more alive than it had ever been, for now it truly was a wounded animal, a mechanical animal with a mind of its own. The *Salamis* fought on.

Chapter XI

On his way back to STC Central Robert Janas carefully watched the glint of metal that followed him in the morning sunlight. Whether it was the same craft that had been with him on his way out to San Francisco the afternoon before he did not know, nor did it matter. The same man or another, his purpose was the same—watch and mark every movement that Robert Janas makes. Nor was Janas sure whom his follower represented, and perhaps that was not significant either. There were two men who would want to know of his activities—Altho Franken of the STC, and Jonal Herrera, Chairman of the Federation. And which of them had sent this man—these men—to follow him did not matter for, in Janas' mind, Franken had come to equal Herrera, Herrera Franken; their goals and purposes matched in this at least.

Swinging down across the mountains Janas brought the grav-car onto the landing deck atop the STC Officer's Hostel. Turning the craft over to an attendant, Janas went into the hostel to his suite, where he shaved and bathed, then to the canteen for a quick breakfast. Returning to his suite he undressed, darkened the room, and climbed into bed.

Late in the afternoon the unconscious clock in his brain awakened him. Shaking the sleep from his eyes Janas called Jarl Emmett and confirmed the meeting to take place at his home that evening. After the call Janas dressed, had supper in the hostel's canteen, and then ordered a hovercab to take him to Emmett's home. He arrived there shortly before twenty o'clock.

There were already better than two dozen people in Emmett's large living room. Some of them Janas knew, most he did not. Among those he recognized were Hal Danser, Juan Kai and Paul D'Lugan. Emmett himself was standing to one side, talking with a tall, slender, dark-haired woman who was probably Janas' senior by half a century.

"Bob," Emmett called across the room, "come here. There's someone I want you to meet."

Janas crossed to the couple.

"Citizeness Syble Dian," Emmett said, "our attorney. This is Bob Janas."

"I'm pleased to meet you," Janas said, shaking her offered hand.

"So you're the infamous Robert Janas," the woman said.

"I guess I am," Janas answered with a smile.

"You look just as I pictured you," she said

"You can take that as a compliment if you want," Emmett said.

"By all means," Syble Dian said. "I meant it that way."

"Thank you."

After a brief, "You're welcome," Citizeness Dian went on: "Do you think you can find a way to get us out of this mess? I'm afraid that there's nothing the *legal* department can do now." She glanced at Paul D'Lugan, the expression on her face seeming to say that he was her antithesis, the "illegal" department.

"I don't know," Janas told her. "I hope so."

By fifteen minutes past twenty, after listening to a private suggestion from Janas, Emmett called the meeting to order.

"First of all," Emmett began, "I want to make sure that none of us have been bugged. Someone has taken a great liking to placing miniature transmitters on us and our friends."

He paused for a moment and let the impact of his words sink in.

"Now," he went on, "I'd like you to go off in pairs, undress, and carefully check your clothing and the clothing of your partner for bugs. Look for any small, regular shaped objects that shouldn't be where you find them. If they can't be identified, destroy them.

"You can use our bedrooms for undressing. Miriam will show you the way."

After a small amount of subdued mumbling, those present accepted Emmett's suggestion and went out to check. The better part of a half hour was consumed in the process.

"Thank you," Emmett said when they had all returned. "I feel a little better now."

Janas noticed that Emmett did not mention the
half dozen or so noisers planted in various spots
around the room. If there were a spy in their midst,
he thought, it would be just as well that he did not
know of the signal disrupting devices.

"Things are coming to a head," Emmett went on to
say. "We all know what Altho Franken has done, the
dangers to which he has exposed the Solar Trading
Company. Well, we have a man with us tonight who
knows those dangers far better than any of the rest of
us."

He paused for a moment, looked at Janas, and then
turned back to his audience.

"Bob Janas is the man who started this organization
and we ought to thank him for it. He was the first to
realize what would happen as the Alliance grew
stronger. He had spent most of his life on the star
worlds and he saw that the rebels could never be
satisfied with merely driving the Federation back to
Earth. If they were ever to be safe they would have to
come to Earth and make the Federation recognize
their sovereignties.

"Bob also realized that the STC would be drawn
into the Rebellion during its last stages, if not before,
and he began to do what he could to see that it stayed
neutral.

"I won't go into everything he's done, but let me
say one thing: Bob has spent a fortune—and risked
his life—to get a set of reports that could save the
STC from destruction. We've got to do everything we
can to see that those reports are used and acted
upon—or Altho Franken and that power hungry mad-

man, Jonal Herrera, will see the whole Spiral Arm destroyed."

A few faces showed shock at Emmett's frank appraisal of the Federation Chairman. Not that it was a criminal offense to speak of him that way, not technically, but the Chairman had his ways of punishing those who spoke against him.

"Bob, will you tell us about your reports?" Emmett said.

Janas stood up, opened his attaché case and took out a duplicate set of the typewritten reports that he had given Altho Franken. He briefly went over the information contained in the reports, elaborating here and there on certain points. There were a few questions asked, mostly academic ones, for by and large the men and women present had already come to the same conclusions—it was suicide for the STC to take sides.

"Tell us what Franken said when you talked with him," Emmett suggested.

Janas lit a cigarette and looked at the others for a moment.

"Franken has made up his mind," he said slowly. "There's nothing anyone can say or do to make him change it. It's that simple."

"Did he read your reports?" one of the men asked.

"No, he gave them to his secretary to read," Janas said. "He was supposed to give Franken a digest of them."

"Milt Anchor?" Syble Dian asked. When Janas nodded, she went on. "Anchor sympathizes with the Federation. He'll do nothing to change Franken's mind."

Several heads nodded in agreement.

"Then what do we do?" Paul D'Lugan asked angrily.

Janas turned to look at the younger man, sensing what he was going to suggest. No one spoke for a few moments.

"You all know it," D'Lugan said. "We don't have any choice now. There's only one way left to save the STC."

He paused as if waiting for someone else to say it.

"I don't like it," Emmett said suddenly.

"Nobody likes it, Jarl," Janas said, "but we can't beat around the bush about it. Mr. D'Lugan is suggesting that we use force against Citizen Franken."

Voices mumbled across the room.

"What I want to know is this," Janas said, "does anyone else have a better idea?"

A smile crept across D'Lugan's face.

"I don't," Janas went on after a while. "I don't like the idea of storming Franken's office by force. I'll do anything I can to avoid it, but if there's no other way . . ." He left it to hang in the air.

"Let's do this," Jarl Emmett suggested. "All of us go home and sleep on it. Go over it again in your minds: the alternatives and the consequences. See if you can come up with something better. Let's not make any rash decisions tonight. Then we'll get together here tomorrow night at the same time and decide. Another twenty-four hours won't make that much difference."

Janas was to remember those words later, but at the moment he only felt relief. A postponement would really solve nothing, but it would give them all a breathing spell, a chance to collect their thoughts a little better, to *maybe* come up with some alternative to a "palace coup" in STC Central.

D'Lugan insisted on deciding then, at that very moment, warning them that Franken might get wind of their plans and take action against them. A majority overruled him and he was forced, under protest, to accept it.

Janas stayed for a few moments after the others left. Sitting on one of Emmett's luxurious couches, a drink in his hand, Janas repeated D'Lugan's warning.

"Really, Jarl," he said, "D'Lugan's no fool. Franken might get wind of what we're doing. You can't rule out a possibility of a spy in the 'Committee.'"

"I know," Emmett agreed. "Franken's tried hard enough to spy on us, if that's who's doing it."

"Don't you think so?"

"Him or Herrera. Six of one, half a dozen of the other, as far as I can see."

"I think you'd better be ready to act," Janas said slowly, "just in case Altho, or whoever, tries to force our hand."

"I've got a couple of tentative plans," Emmett said, "if we have to act. Everyone's briefed on them but you. They're mostly Paul's ideas, but he's good at that sort of thing."

"I suspect he would be," Janas said with a smile. "I'm glad he's on our side."

"Sometimes I wonder," Emmett replied with a similar smile. "Oh, I don't mean I think he may be the spy."

"I know what you mean. What's eating at him anyway?"

"I'm not sure," Emmett said. "He's never told me, but I think he had some relatives on Antigone, brother and his family or something. And then the Federation shot up his ship in '77. He thinks it was on purpose."

"He's not the only one who has that idea."

"I know," Emmett replied. "He's got a lot of hatred inside him, and Altho's a good one to take it out on."

"Tell me about the plans," Janas said, sitting back on the couch and sipping his drink.

The hour was late when he finally took leave of the Emmett family, dozens of ideas swarming in his mind. He climbed into the waiting hovercab and rode back to the Officer's Hostel.

Chapter XII

Seven and a half parsecs from Earth, in the direction where the constellation Aquila lies, a battle raged. The fleets of the Federation had met the rebels—and were being pushed back.

Within the power hungry vacuum called Nonspace, great behemoths of steel tore at each other. Sheets of flame flickered on force screens. Nuclear missiles exploded like tiny novas. Men died as starships became fragments of burning metal and flaming gas. But the battle raged on.

The greatest warship ever put to space by Earth, the mighty *Salamis,* was torn in a dozen places. There was no longer any living thing within her, at least not living in the sense that men live, but there was still a mind aboard her, a mind whose brain was made of transistors and ultra-microminiature integrated circuit modules, of relays and ferrite cores—and that mind fought on.

Her protecting force screen flickered and faded ominously, yet always came back to full power in time to intercept missiles or energy blasts that could have destroyed her. In turn she gave back the fire, opening her screens for fractions of nanoseconds to allow her own missiles and energy blasts to speed toward their destinations.

Again and again the enemy hemmed her in, hammered at her screens, poured nuclear flame into her discharge banks, sought to break down her shield, to get past her defenses and reduce her to vapor and fragments. And again and again she held them off, destroying them, driving them back, then falling away, fighting a delaying action as, coexistent light-year by light-year, coexistent parsec by parsec, the Federation fleet slowly yielded to the rebels.

Then, at last, the inevitable happened. A stronger force of the enemy encircled the *Salamis,* cutting her off from aid, lashing at her, so loading her force screens that she could no longer absorb the energy. Her screens flamed up brightly. She glowed like a tiny star, illuminating space around her for thousands of kilometers—then they failed. The most powerful force screens ever built into a warship burst and the wall of energy around the *Salamis* imploded, rushed in toward a common center, the *Salamis* herself.

The tiny star flamed brighter still—her nuclear engines vanished—matter became energy—energy passed through itself and then exploded outward. The *Salamis* ceased to be.

A cheer went up from the rebel forces. They had beaten the best the Federation had to throw against them. They pushed forward. The Federation lines broke, turned tail, fled toward Earth.

The rebels followed—this battle, at least, was over. Earth lay before them.

Aboard his flagship, the heavy battle crusier *Guadalcanal*, General Henri Kantralas wept, but whether out of sadness or gratitude, no man knew.

Chapter XIII

Sleep did not come easily to Robert Janas on the night of the meeting at Jarl Emmett's home. Slowly, reluctantly, he was coming to the conclusion that there was no other choice open to the "conspirators." If they did sincerely believe that the STC's only hope lay in neutrality then they had no choice but to do what they could to save it—even if that meant violence against the person of the president of the corporation, against Altho Franken, who had been Janas' friend for more decades than he liked to remember.

Lying naked on the bed, physically tired but mentally wide awake, too many questions in his mind, Janas found himself oddly introspective, oddly indecisive.

In an age when government totalitarianism grew stronger by the day, Robert Janas had been raised to believe certain ancient ideals, the morals and ethics of the culture that had built the Solar Trading Company and opened the paths to the stars. Janas' father had taught him well: the only moral relationships between men are those of a purely voluntary nature. Men must come together, his father had said, of their own free will and contract between themselves.

No man must use force, Janas believed without ever really consciously expressing it before, unless it was first used against him, and then only to defend himself, to free himself of what other men would cause him to do against his will, against his own rational judgment. "To initiate the use of force is a moral abomination."

Can we, Janas asked himself, a deeper part of his mind observing him, wondering about this uncharacteristic hesitation, asking what it was that made him stop and deliberate so long on this course of action, that caused him a sort of moral uncertainty that he had not known in many years . . . Can we use violence against Franken? Or in doing so will we become no better than he is? Does *this* end justify *this* means?

Into Janas' mind flashed a scene of the major city of Odin, the streets of University filled with raging mobs, flames devouring the greatest citadel of learning in mankind's history, Federation soldiers murdering, raping, plundering, destroying—and the citizens of Odin striking back at the Federation with murder, rape, plunder and destruction. They were—had been —honest, decent people, men and women who had believed as Janas believed, driven by the oppression of the Federation, goaded by their own zealots, into striking back with the only weapons at hand, and in that process destroying themselves and the very things they had sought to defend.

It is not they who have initiated the use of force, Janas told himself, lying there in the darkness, gazing at the faint sparkles of light thrown against the ceiling through the unpolarized window. It is the Federation, and that decades ago. It is the Federation and the men who lead it, the growing power of the tyrants of the past thirty or forty decades, who had initiated the violence, who have declared to themselves the right to coerce and use force. It is the Federation that has violated men's rights, that has demanded that men act against their own judgments. It is the Federation itself that is outlaw, not the rebels who seek to destroy it.

And Franken? Janas asked himself. What of him? In allying himself with the Federation he has accepted their code of morality, he has made himself one with them and agreed that men do have the right to force other men to do *their* will. In that, Franken has accepted their guilt. In that, Franken has joined those who have initiated the use of force—and we have the right, if not the moral obligation, to return force with force, to take action against Altho Franken himself.

Janas stopped and asked himself: is this reason or merely rationalisation? Have I started with a conclusion and worked backward to build a framework to support it?

In the darkness he again visualised the horror and death in the streets of Odin and told himself that he was right, that the Odinese were right, that even the rebels—or at least General Kantralas—were right. The STC must be stopped from siding with the Federation—and destroying itself. Force *must* be used against Altho Franken.

It was still dark when he drifted off to sleep, though dawn was not long in coming.

*

The breakfast hour was long past when Janas finally awoke, so he called the desk and asked that a glass of juice and a cup of coffee be delivered to his suite. While he waited he looked out again at the bald peak of Mount Union, at the grim reminder of nuclear war and what it had done nearly a millennium and a half ago. That specter still haunted him. It wouldn't be the same now, he knew. Things had changed since that ancient war. Now men had force screens to deflect the nuclear flame, energy cannon to stop the missiles still hundreds of kilometers away—but the bombs were bigger now, terribly bigger, and energy cannon could blast through force screens—and whole planets (smoldering Antigone) could be incinerated. One bomb, of sufficient size, could turn half the Colorado Plateau into a molten bed of lava, and where would that leave mankind a thousand years from now?

Just before he turned away from the window Janas saw the weekly tour boat coming in from Flagstaff, making a wide swing around Central, letting the tourists get one grand, overall view of the STC city before landing in the central field and plunging them into the panorama of the past, the commercial history of the last twelve hundred years. As the big lumbering chopper settled in the field Janas fought against wondering about the tourists of the future; would they come to see the Great Arizonal Abyss?

You're getting old, Robert Janas, he told himself just before the boy brought his coffee and juice. The century mark has done something to you, taken the fight out of you. Snap out of it!

Over his coffee and first cigarette of the morning, he reviewed the structure of the Solar Trading Com-

pany. He sketched out the chain of command on a
piece of paper, the flow by which Altho Franken's
orders had gone out to the STC starships, ordering
them to give aid to the Federation.

Altho, president, stood at the top of the pyramid.
He was, in theory, responsible to the Board of Directors, though in practice his hands were free to do as
he chose as long as he could justify his actions as
being in the best interest of the corporation. Since, at
the present time, the Board was composed primarily of
Franken's relatives and supporters, there was little
chance of overruling him through that body. However
there was an alternative course available.

Below Franken came a raft of vice presidents,
twelve in number, each responsible for one major
division of the corporation. The most important of
these, at least from Janas' viewpoint, was the Vice
President in Charge of Operations, Bilthor Franken,
Altho's older brother, whom Janas knew but slightly.
He was, so Janas understood, an honest, hard working
man with little imagination, who followed his dynam-
ic younger brother's orders with little question. Under
him came Jarl Emmett, Operations Supervisor, the
man who saw to the implementation of the decisions
and orders of Bilthor Franken. When the orders had
gone out for the STC to aid the Federation Emmett
had known of them, but had been unable to prevent
them.

It was Operations that scheduled the activities of
the STC star fleets, that saw to it that the starships
did what they were supposed to do, were where they
were meant to be when they were meant to be there.
And it was through Operations that the orders would
have to be withdrawn—though Emmett had as little

power in this as he had had in preventing the issuance of those original orders.

Stated quite simply the problem was this: to prevent the STC from actually giving aid to the Federation, Emmett, Janas and the others would have to (one) gain control of Altho Franken and his brother Bilthor, (two) get them both to sign an emergency priority corporate policy change which would bypass the Board of Directors, and (three) see that countermanding orders were issued to the Operations computer. It was that simple.

"Simple!" Janas said to himself with a smile.

It was almost noon when Janas rose from the desk, wadded his notes and dropped them into the desktop disintegrator. He did not hear the "puff" that indicated that the papers had been consumed, but it did not register at the time. He shaved, slipped into a clean uniform, and went to the canteen.

The canteen was nearly filled with tourists from the boat he had seen earlier, but he soon found an empty, fairly secluded corner and sat down. Slipping his Taste Preference card into the menu, he waited until the screen lighted and then began scanning the offerings. He noted the absence of Raman fleshflower, which he had intended to order. He attributed this to the war which had restricted the importation of many items and passed on to the classic Terran roast beef.

An attractive waitress brought him his apéritif only moments after the menu clicked his TP card back into his hand. Thanking her, he sat back in his chair and refused to think about anything more significant than the glass of wine in his hand.

With gratifying promptness his meal was brought to him. Thanking the pretty waitress again, he dug into the steaming platter before him. He was even hungrier than he had thought.

So intent was he on his meal that he did not notice the two strangers who approached his table.

"Captain Janas?" the question was asked.

Janas looked up to see a dark, handsome young man whose face was somehow vaguely familiar. To the young man's left stood a tall, nicely built, very pretty young blonde—the name "Rinni" immediately came to his mind.

"Do you mind if we sit down, captain?" the girl asked.

After only a moment's hesitation, Janas replied: "No, please do."

"Thank you," they both answered, drawing chairs away from the table and seating themselves. For a moment no one spoke.

Up close Rinni and Gray, the so-called Moondog Dancers from Eddie's in Flagstaff of two nights before, were just as handsome a couple as they had appeared to be on stage, though now, of course, they were fully dressed, if Earth's costumes could be called dress.

Rinni wore an open-front blouse, several strands of pearls, a half meter length skirt and kid boots. Her golden hair was piled high on her head in a conical fashion. Gray was dressed in what Janas had come to accept as normal garb among the Earthmen; a skin-tight suit of blue and gold, a peaked golden cap and pale blue, pointed boots.

"You don't have to introduce yourselves," Janas said between mouthfulls. "I know who you are."

The couple looked at each other briefly.

"I caught your show in Eddie's night before last," he told them.

"Oh," Rinni said, her red mouth forming an almost perfect circle.

"Did you like it?" Gray asked.

"It was good," Janas said smiling, "very good in fact, but you aren't from Odin."

"No, we're not," Rinni said, her voice reminding Janas of the tinkling bells of Rama, played by the wind in a tiny, tree-protected shrine. "We were both born on Earth but I grew up on Telemachus. My mother was from there."

"That's in the Cluster," Gray said, "about . . "

"I know," Janas said. "About eighteen lights from Odin, toward the galactic center."

"You've spent a lot of time in the Cluster, haven't you?" Gray asked.

Janas nodded.

There was silence again.

"What do you want?" Janas asked at last, spacing his words carefully. They certainly weren't the tourists they apparently wished to appear to be. They may have come in on the tour boat, he thought, but that wasn't their real reason for coming here; I was. Why?

Rinni briefly opened the purse she carried by a shoulder strap. Inside Janas caught a brief glimpse of a military issue noiser, its pilot light glowing brightly in the shadows of the purse's interior. He nodded understanding.

"We're both registered as Earth natives, licensed entertainers," Rinni said, her voice suddenly firmer, less that of the merely pretty girl she had seemed to be. "We can come and go pretty much as we please and no one asks questions. We even performed before the Chairman himself last month in Geneva."

Gray made an unpleasant face and Janas could

guess the reason for it. Jonal Herrera was, among other things, known for his fondness for pretty women.

"And you're agents of the Alliance of Independent Worlds," Janas said slowly, more of a statement than a question.

"We are," Rinni replied.

"What do you want with me?" Janas asked again.

"We know exactly who you are, captain," Rinni said, "and exactly why you are on Earth."

"You do," Janas said flatly, refusing to allow his voice to show his feelings, which were primarily a sense of annoyance at too many people prying into the doings of Robert Janas. This was overlaid with a mild distrust of the two young strangers. They wanted something from him—he thought he knew what it was—and he was not about to align himself with another faction. Settling the STC's problems was a big enough job.

"What did Altho Franken say when you told him to keep the STC out of the war?" Rinni asked.

"Don't you know that too?"

Rinni smiled a tight smile, the hard-boiled mask slipping just slightly from her face.

"We have a pretty good idea," Gray answered.

"You're probably right too," Janas said.

"What do you intend to do about it, captain?" Rinni asked, the mask coming back over her fine features.

"What business is it of yours?"

"We want to help you," Rinni said.

"Captain Janas," Gray said with all the feeling of his youth, "General Kantralas doesn't want to destroy the STC. He is more than willing to accept its neutrality. He knows that the STC is really his friend."

"Altho Franken isn't his friend," Janas said.

"Are you?" asked Rinni, her blue eyes flashing.

"In a manner of speaking," Janas said. "I agree with him on certain points and I certainly don't want the STC to join in fighting him."

"He who is not against us . . ." Gray began.

"Wait a minute," Janas said, raising his hand. "Exactly what are you getting at?"

"You and your friends are working for the same things we are," Rinni told him.

"And what is that?" Janas demanded.

"The destruction of the Federation," Rinni said, a note of puzzlement in her voice. "An end to these terrible decades of war. The freedom of all worlds from the domination of Earth. The establishment of a universal and just peace." She paused for a moment, looking at Janas. "Mankind can no longer tolerate the brutality and atrocities of Chairman Herrera."

"The Federation isn't the only one who has committed atrocities," Janas said slowly. "What about Cassandra and Erda? Have you forgotten about them?"

"Have you forgotten about Antigone and Odin, captain?" Rinni asked. "Atrocity and genocide are a matter of Federation policy. We didn't begin it."

"But you continued it," Janas told her.

"Only in self-defense, captain." There was real anger in Rinni's voice. "And with us it isn't a matter of policy. Our leaders did not *order* it, did not condone it."

"Have the men who led the raids on Cassandra and Erda been punished?" Janas asked.

"No," Rinni answered, "but that's no indication that we approve of what they did. We can't afford to lose any of our leaders. They may have been wrong in the way they accomplished their goals but they were still acting, so they believed, in the best interests of the Alliance."

Janas was silent for a moment.

"That's minor, sir," Gray said. "I mean, that's beside the main point. We both want the end of Herrera's tyranny and an open, honest alliance of worlds, each one free, equal and sovereign. The whole Spiral Arm's sick of one man, one planet domination. We're all working toward that end."

Janas shook his head slowly. "You may have misunderstood my aims," he said. "My aspirations are a little more modest than yours."

"And what are your aspirations, captain?" Rinni asked, her voice as hard and cold as steel, no bell-like sound there.

"All I want is to see the STC stay clear," he told her. "I don't really hope to be able to accomplish anything more than that and there's some doubt about our being able to do that."

Neither Rinni nor Gray spoke for a few moments.

"We agree on that point, Captain Janas," Gray said after a while.

"I suppose we do," Janas agreed, taking the last bite of his beef. "In fact I agree in principle with your desires. I just don't think they're very realistic under the present circumstances."

"What do you mean, captain?" Jinni asked.

"You seem to think that all you have to do is slay a dragon named the Terran Federation and we can all live happily ever after. I'm afraid it's not that easy."

"Go on," Rinni said.

"When it's over, assuming that you win, what are you going to do with the monsters you've created? How are you going to eliminate men like Carman Dubourg from the picture? He's building his own little empire while he helps you knock Herrera's apart. He's not going to join in your 'free and equal' alliance.

"And what are you going to do about planets like Erda and Cassandra? Do you think they'll ever join your alliance or even come to terms with you people after what you've done to them? It's just not that easy," he said again.

"Please continue, captain," Rinni said, her voice a hoarse whisper. "I think I'm beginning to understand you."

"No, you're not," Janas said, shaking his head. "And I won't say anything more. You believe in what you're doing and I suppose I admire you for it. I really do hope you *can* create the kind of world you're dreaming of."

"You don't think we can win, is that what you mean?" Gray asked.

"I don't think anyone can win," Janas said "I only *hope* that the STC can survive."

"As I said, captain, we agree on that point," Gray said. "We can at least work together to accomplish that."

"No," Janas said, "I won't join you and I don't want you joining us. This is a family matter, for the STC only."

"Captain," Rinni said, having held her anger in check, "we could be of great help to you if you'd let us. We have a powerful organization here on Earth, far more powerful than you may realise."

"Thanks, but no thanks!" Janas told her.

"There's nothing we can do?" Gray asked hopelessly.

Janas was silent for a moment. "Do you have people in San Francisco?"

"Yes," Gray answered.

"There are two things I'd like for your people to check on," Janas said. "One of them's a personal matter, but the other—well, it's up to you."

"Tell us," Rinni said crisply.

"There's an organization called 'The Sons of Liberty' or something like that. They're planning to assassinate Herrera. They're a bunch of damned fools, but maybe you can use them for something." He gave them Rod Campbell's address.

"We'll look into it," Rinni said.

"The other . . ." Janas said. "There's a girl I would like someone to keep an eye on. It would be of great help to me. I would be able to devote myself more fully to our mutual goal."

The young couple looked at each other.

"Yes," Gray answered for them, "I suppose we could do something like that. Who is it?"

After Janas had quickly told them of Enid he offered to buy them each a drink.

"No, thank you, captain," Rinni replied. "The tour boat will be going back to Flagstaff soon and we'd better be on it. If we stay away any longer our absence may be noticed."

"I'm sorry that things didn't work out as you planned," Janas said.

"We understand," Gray said, though his expression did not seem to indicate it.

"If you change your mind, captain," Rinni said as they rose, "you know where to find us."

"I know."

"Good bye, captain," Rinni said for them both.

Janas watched them walk away, admiring the gentle sway of Rinni's hips. Quite a girl, he thought, not quite sure of what he meant by it.

He waited a few minutes, sipping an almost cold cup of coffee, before rising and paying his check. He went directly back toward his suite, stopping only long enough to buy a carton of cigarettes from a machine.

As he got off the elevator and went down the hallway toward the suite that had been allotted him, he felt a strange, unpleasant sensation, a premonition, he might have said, had it come that close to consciousness. Something nagged at his mind, but he found himself unable to pin it down and say exactly what it was. He shrugged, lit a cigarette, and went toward his suite.

As he thumbed the door open a series of apparently disjointed events came to him. The desk disintegrator—it had not consumed the papers. Whoever had been shadowing him since his arrival on Earth was no longer there. At the meeting the night before both he and Emmett had spoken against the Chairman of the Federation, and had, he supposed, openly committed themselves to criminal conspiracy. And, he felt suddenly, the elevator and the hallway were too empty, too quiet.

He stopped, then snatched his thumb away from the door scanner—but it was too late. The automatics had opened it and he stood looking into the room, at the bulky figures of two Solar Trading Company Pinkers, security men in their harsh, black uniforms.

"Captain Robert Janas?" asked the senior of the two Pinkers, holding in his hand an official looking piece of paper.

Janas swallowed the lump in his throat.

"Yes," he said hollowly.

"You are under arrrest, sir," the Pinker said.

"What for?"

"You will be notified in due time, sir," the officer said politely. "Will you come with us quietly?"

Chapter XIV

Sixteen and a half light-years from Sol, lying near the plane of the ecliptic as seen from Earth, is a star called Alpha Aquilae, Altair to the ancients. White-hot, with a surface temperature in the neighborhood of 11,000°C, an A7 star, eleven times brighter than Sol, Altair beamed its heat and light into the planetless void around it.

In another universe, at a spot that coincided with that of Altair if one were to bridge the gap between universes through the heart of that star, a fleet of starships fled for its life through the grayness.

It was a complete disaster; a total rout. The mightiest star fleet that Earth could muster had met the enemy and had been defeated. The *Salamis* had gone down heroically, but when she did go down nearly half the effective strength of the Federation's armada had gone with her. The ships had inflicted great damage upon the rebels also: it had been a costly victory for those who challenged the Federation's authority, a cost they could ill afford to pay—but they had won; they had defeated the Federation's armada, and while that shattered fleet fled toward the doubtful sanctuary of Earth, the rebels pushed on toward Sol and the heart of the Federation itself.

Battered, seared, leaking air in a thousand places, her crew bloody but still aware, still fighting, the Federation flagship *Shilo* limped Earthward. Her captain and Abli Juliene conferred. Before them was a large 3-V projection tank inside which were displayed the stars of the local section of the galaxy and bright points of red and green light—red for the enemy, green for the Federation. Red lights outnumbered green as they fled, red behind green, toward a blinking point of blue light, Earth. The Grand Admiral slowly opened a packet—orders only to be opened in case of defeat. His face was tired and lined and looked old, terribly old.

For a few moments Grand Admiral Juliene stood reading his orders, then silently handed them over to the *Shilo's* captain. He looked into the pseudo-depths of the 3-V tank and shook his graying head sadly. Then he took a small note pad from his blouse pocket and began writing.

The *Shilo's* captain did not speak, waiting for the admiral to say the first word, but the admiral remained quiet. He silently handed the scribbled notes to the captain, sighed, charged and lit an old brier pipe, and began to slowly pace the deck.

Well you showed me up again, Henri, he thought. Maybe I should have listened to you, maybe I should have pulled out when you did and gone in with the rebels. At least we'd be fighting on the same side. But I thought I knew better then. I thought I'd play the cards as they'd been dealt me and try to make the best of it.

He looked down at his hands. How does it feel, Henri? How do you get the blood off? You've got it on your hands the same as me, the blood of all those innocent people. Mine is from Antigone and Odin and God only knows how many more. It's mine; I gave the orders; I've got to accept it. And the blood of all those boys who died out there today.

But you've got your own blood, Henri. You've got Cassandra and Erda and some others. You've got the blood of innocents on your hands, too, and how do we get it off? How do we ever sleep again at night?

Oh, God, Henri, he cried to himself, what have we done to mankind?

The *Shilo*'s captain had crossed the large compartment and tapped a button that alerted the communications officer and said: "Prepare a capsule. For Earth. There's a message coming through." Then he inserted the admiral's notes into a device that transmitted a copy of them to the communications officer. That done the captain looked back at the 3-V tank, and he, like the Grand Admiral, sighed sadly.

*

Below decks the communications officer saw to it that a message capsule was readied at once and the admiral's handwritten notes placed inside it. Then the capsule was kicked outside the ship, where it fired a powerful plasma jet and began accelerating into the grayness of Non-space, toward a spot where a world called Earth lay in a coexistent universe.

The capsule sped faster and faster, accelerating at a rate that would have reduced human flesh and bone to little more than jelly smeared thinly on the rear bulkheads, and at that ever increasing speed rushed toward the locality of Earth.

A few hours after leaving the *Shilo* the message capsule reached a complex of structures roughly coexistent with the orbit of Saturn. By then it had slowed its speed, and it finally came to a dead stop within a few kilometers of the Non-space station, emitting an alerting signal. In response to the signal the station swept out a tractor beam, locked in on the capsule, and transferred it to a Jump Unit hanging freely in Non-space, energized and at potential. The capsule passed through the unit's field and squirted through flawed space into the continuum of stars.

A crew of men, working under the bright stars of the galaxy, out where Sol was a shrunken, wan disk, opened the capsule, removed its contents and fed them into a scanning device. The Grand Admiral's notes were translated into electronic pulses and relayed to Earth, then nearly ten and a half astronomical units away. Something near one hour and twenty-nine minutes had passed before the signal reached Luna from where it was relayed to the Chief Signal Officer of the Federation in the city of Geneva. Once received the message was decoded, then immediately relayed to the office of the Chairman.

Eight hours and fourteen minutes after the Grand Admiral scrawled his message on the note pad an almost exact duplicate of those notes came out of a machine built into the desk of Jonal Herrera, Chairman of the Federation.

The most powerful human being in the galaxy sat looking at the half dozen sheets of paper, the thin, wavy lines that spoke of the destruction of the mightiest armada in human history—and that man came as close to weeping as he ever had in his adult life.

Chapter XV

Janas was too stunned to speak at first. He had never seriously considered that the Pinkers might arrest him, though now he fully realized that he was, in fact, involved in a "criminal" conspiracy. And, too, he realized how blundering and inept had been those leading the conspiracy; how amateurish and obvious had been the actions of himself, of Jarl Emmett and the others. Franken had known, even when Janas went to see him on that first day back on Earth, that there was a movement afoot to call back his orders to the STC star fleets—a movement that was willing, if reluctant, to take steps beyond mere talking. He had only been waiting until they had committed themselves, until the "committee," the night before, had tentatively and tremulously discussed the use of force, had spoken against the august office of the Chairman of the Terran Federation. A spy in their midst, while not able to electronically record the conversation, could still testify against them, evidence damning enough for a Federation court of law to convict Robert Janas and Jarl Emmett, along with the others, of criminal conspiracy. Then Altho had acted, with the Chairman's blessing. Janas cursed himself for a fool and stood helpless, unarmed before the Pinkers.

"I'll come," he said at last, wondering how good were his chances of escape, and wondering too what he would do were he able to escape, where he would go on this world that was no longer his own.

"This way, sir," the senior of the Pinkers said politely, gesturing for Janas to go down the hall toward the elevator.

Quietly he obeyed, though keeping alert for an opening that might give him the opportunity to act.

It happened quickly, Janas' escape from the two young Pinkers who were too easy going, too careless. They did not dream of violence here in officer country of the STC Hostel.

One moment the hallway before and behind was quiet, empty; the next a dark, curly-headed young man seemed to appear out of nowhere, a stunner in his hand.

"Hit it, Janas!" he yelled as the stunner buzzed.

Janas recognized the newcomer as Paul D'Lugan, and acted. Leaping backward with his arms outspread, Janas knocked both Pinkers off balance. One stumbled against the wall, his hand grabbing for the stunner on his hip, but he was too slow—the beam of paralysing energy from D'Lugan's weapon reached his body, passed through the flesh of his abdomen, found the nerve complex of his spine, and the astonished Pinker collapsed.

As D'Lugan brought down one, Janas jerked the second guard off his feet and threw him savagely against the wall. Jumping forward, his right elbow leading his body, Janas slammed into the Pinker, sinking his elbow in the younger man's soft throat. The security officer released a strangled groan, flailed his arms in an attempt to throw the starship captain away. Moving back just enough to give himself room to swing Janas threw his right fist into the Pinker's stomach, his left into his descending chin.

The man who had come to arrest Janas gurgled painfully and fell limp to the carpeted hallway.

"Hurry," D'Lugan cried, shoving the stunner into his belt and grabbing the nearer of the unconscious security officers, "let's get them into your suite."

In a few moments, both breathing hard, Janas and D'Lugan had the two limp forms inside the suite, tied in strips of bed sheet, and unceremoniously stuffed into a closet.

"They ought to be out for a while," D'Lugan said.

"What are you doing here?" Janas asked when his voice came back to him.

"I'll give you a full report later," D'Lugan replied. "We don't have time for it now. Jarl's still free and holding Operations. Have you got any 'civies'?"

"Yes," Janas answered.

"Earth-style?" D'Lugan asked, jerking a thumb toward his own garish costume.

"No," Janas told him, forcing a smile.

"I've got some for you." D'Lugan ducked out of the suite for a moment, and then returned with a package. "They're your size," he said, offering the package to Janas.

Inside he found a bright red and white striped shirt with loose sleeves, lace collar and cuffs, harlequin pants of gold and purple with a startlingly white, grotesquely padded codpiece, red boots and a peaked felt cap of the same purple as the pants. He looked for a moment at the wild clothing, then looked at D'Lugan's, which was no better, and decided that on Earth the quiet sobriety of his STC uniform was probably more conspicuous in a crowd than what D'Lugan was offering him.

"Don't be squeamish, captain," D'Lugan said, a smile breaking across his face. "It makes me sick, too, but that's what the well-dressed man wears on this crazy planet. 'When in Rome,' and all that crap."

Janas returned the smile, suddenly finding that he liked D'Lugan—not so much for his startling rescue but because he had a degree of taste that Earth seemed to have forgotten. D'Lugan was a starman like himself, a ship's officer, and perhaps—no, probably, from what Jarl Emmett had said—he had ample reason for hating Altho Franken and what he had come to represent.

Without answering Janas stripped and then dressed in the gaudy clothing. Delaying D'Lugan for a moment, he took tissue copies of the two reports from his attaché case and stuffed them inside his shirt. He turned to go into the bedroom.

"Hurry up," D'Lugan snapped. "We don't have much time."

"Just a minute," Janas answered. Opening one of his suitcases, he took out a dark, heavy metal object, the traditional side arm of STC captains. It was a twentieth century, old style, weapon, a militant and obviously deadly .45 caliber automatic pistol, a weapon to which Janas owed his life several times over. He slipped the pistol inside his shirt, hoping that its bulk would not be too obvious within the loose folds, grabbed a handful of shells from a box in the suitcase, dropped them into a pocket, and then left with D'Lugan.

"Where are we going?" he asked as the door slid closed behind them.

"To pay a social call," D'Lugan said. "Just stay with me and try not to look too obvious."

Without speaking again the younger man led Janas to the nearest grav-elevator. They rode down several floors, got off, took stairs down two or three flights, boarded another elevator and rode to the buildings's basement levels. Getting out again D'Lugan led a meandering course through several floors of the sub-surface levels, up stairs to the ground floor, across the hostel's lobby, where stood half a dozen Pinkers who only glanced casually in their direction, and then outside the building.

D'Lugan spoke only once, and then to say: "We're going there." He was pointing toward the beautifully imposing Graham Franken building where Altho Franken had his offices.

Janas felt annoyance at D'Lugan's commanding at-titude but admitted to himself that the younger man knew what the plan was, and he didn't. Later he would have an opportunity to learn just what was happening and why.

Without incident they entered the Graham Frank-en building, crossed the huge main lobby, rode es-calators and elevators until they at last arrived at the upper levels and the offices of the STC hierarchy, to the huge reception room where Janas had come two days before seeking audience with Altho.

Unhesitatingly the younger man crossed to one of the receptionists, the very girl with whom Janas had spoken before. The girl looked up. A startled expres-sion went across her face, and the single word "Paul" involuntarily broke from her lips.

"The show is on," D'Lugan said softly.

Something that might have been fear went across the girl's face, then it was gone. She glanced around nervously, looked at Janas with recognition, then back to D'Lugan.

"May I help you, sir?" she asked, her voice nearly normal now, and loud enough for others to hear.

D'Lugan glanced at Janas and winked heavily.

"We are Citizens Hendricks and Malheim," D'Lugan said. "We have an appointment with Citizen Altho Franken."

The girl's head nodded almost imperceptibly and there was understanding within her green eyes. She punched a button on the desk before her, or at least gave a convincing imitation of doing so.

"Citizen Franken will see you in a few moments," she said after having seemed to listen to a reply from someone. "Please have a seat and I'll call you."

As they crossed to the luxurious waiting room chairs D'Lugan whispered four words that seemed sufficient explanation: "Maura is with us."

He did not speak again.

Janas fumbled in the awkward pockets of his new outfit and discovered that he had forgotten to bring cigarettes with him in the rush to leave his suite. D'Lugan seemed to recognize the predicament, drew a pack from his own pocket, and offered one to Janas. The starship captain accepted gratefully.

As he puffed the cigarette to life and scanned the large waiting room, Janas felt terribly open, obvious and conspicuous, though he realized that this was probably the last place that the Pinkers would think to look for them, and it did not seem likely that any of the receptionists, other than Maura, would recognize him. Here he and D'Lugan were fairly safe—for a short while at least—and it was obvious that D'Lugan did not plan for them to stay long in the open. Maura was involved and it appeared that D'Lugan expected her to actually get them into Altho Franken's office.

Well, Janas asked himself, isn't that the logical thing to do? We have no choice now if we expect to accomplish anything, no choice other than direct action. And Altho Franken's office seems like the best place to take that action.

He felt the heavy bulk of the .45 inside his shirt and that comforted him some, though it did not relieve the uneasy sensation of being watched. He was sure that the short hair on the back of his neck was standing on end, but doubted that anyone would notice *that*.

Janas had almost finished the cigarette when the receptionist called for them. In a voice just slightly louder than normal she said: "Citizens Hendricks and Malheim, Citizen Franken will see you now. Please follow me."

Careful not to act too quickly, Janas rose to his feet with D'Lugan. The two of them followed the girl across the reception room and into the long corridor that led toward Franken's private suite of offices.

Once sufficiently distant from the reception room the girl stopped and turned a questioning look toward D'Lugan.

"Yes," he answered her, "we're going to Altho's office." He turned to Janas. "Captain Robert Janas, Maura Biela."

"We've met," Janas said.

"I wasn't sure the other day," Maura said. "I thought you were the same man Paul had spoken of."

"We don't have time for small talk," D'Lugan said, pulling his stunner from the hidden pocket inside his shirt. "Take this." He placed the weapon in Janas' hand.

"What do you want me to do?" Janas asked.

"Wait here," D'Lugan replied. "Give us about a minute, then follow. I'll distract Anchor. You come up and stun him before he has a chance to do anything. Okay?"

Janas nodded.

D'Lugan patted the girl's shoulder and then gave her a gentle shove. They went off down the corridor and Janas stood silently counting off the seconds to himself.

When the minute had passed he glanced around, saw no one in either direction, and followed.

Rounding the last corner, Janas heard D'Lugan's voice talking loudly.

"Look, citizen," he was saying. "Citizen Franken is expecting me. Don't fool around any longer."

"Sir," Anchor protested, "I have not been so informed. He is busy now. I cannot ..."

"There has been some kind of mistake, Citizen Anchor," Maura said. "I have authorization from ..."

Janas listened no longer. He stepped forward, swinging up the stunner and aiming toward Anchor's face. The dark young secretary looked up in astonishment, leaped forward to push a button on his desk. The stunner in Janas' hand buzzed angrily and Anchor's movements disintegrated into an ungraceful collapse across the desk. D'Lugan grabbed his limp form and threw it to the floor.

"Give it to me," D'Lugan said, gesturing toward the stunner. Janas threw it to him and snatched the .45 from inside his shirt. A savagely pleasant feeling of having at last begun to act filled him as he stepped beside D'Lugan before the large double doors that led into Franken's office.

"Open it," D'Lugan said across his shoulder to Maura who now stood behind the desk, reaching for the button that gave access to the official suite.

There was almost total silence as the doors slid apart, revealing the inside of the room and Altho Franken, sitting at his desk, peering intently at a large map spread out before him. Standing beside the desk, his back to the doors, was a Pinker officer, a grizzled old warrior with a needle pistol on his hip and bright piping on his uniform.

For an instant Franken was silent, studying something the officer indicated on the map, then suddenly he seemed to realize that the doors were no longer closed.

"What is it, Milt?" he asked as he looked up. When he saw the two armed men in the doorway his face went white.

The Pinker officer, long years of training and experience apparently moving him without his conscious thought, spun, his big right hand dropping to the needler on his hip.

"Bob," Franken gasped, then broke from his shock and reached for something under his desk.

Needle pistol clearing holster the Pinker leaped aside, swinging his hand up to aim even as he moved. Tracking him like a radar-controlled energy cannon, Janas' .45 blasted, its flash unexpectedly bright, its noise echoing from the room's walls.

The spinning metal slug reached the Pinker just as he depressed the firing stud of his needler, tearing into the colorful decorations that adorned the left breast of his uniform blouse, knocking him backward, a gurgling gasp from his open mouth, a shocked expression on his face. The needler feebly sputtered once, then fell from his dying hand. The security officer continued to stagger backward, his mouth working soundlessly. Then he fell back across the carpet and lay quietly.

D'Lugan's stunner had buzzed and Altho Franken slumped forward across his desk, one limp hand knocking over a tall glass. The amber liquid spilled across the map and dripped off onto the lush carpeting.

Chapter XVI

The iron will and strength of personality that had put him where he was came to the rescue of the Chairman of the Terran Federation. He had never been the sort of man to cry over spilt milk—or blood. What was done was done, and the most any man could do was make the best of an unpleasant situation, salvage whatever he could.

Chairman Herrera slowly, carefully reread the notes sent to him by the commander of the defeated fleet. Juliene had always really expected to be beaten, he said to himself, but he was the best I had. Once again he read them, then tapped a button on his desk and informed an aide to have copies sent to the Speaker of the Parliament, the Chief of the General Staff, the Commandant of the Lunar Garrison, and to the President of the Solar Trading Company.

Herrera sat quietly for a moment thinking about that last one, Al Franken, wondering just how dependable he was. Oh, certainly, Franken had given his word, but was he any more true to his word than—well, than Herrera himself would be? And what about that man—Janas, his name was—could Franken really handle him and his followers? Herrera wondered if it had been wise to allow Franken to control the matter. Maybe he should have had Janas picked up by Federal men. But then, he thought, his spy in Janas' group, actually a double-agent that Franken thought to be in *his* pay exclusively, had advised that it would cause far less trouble with the touchy STC if they were allowed to handle it themselves, and Herrera wanted as little trouble from the STC right now as he could manage. His agent, this spy who was in the very midst of the conspiracy, had sworn that Franken would not send a countermanding order, no matter what pressure Janas put on him—a needle beam would see to that if need be.

Yes, Herrera said to himself, we'll let Franken handle this—for now. The STC is a proud bunch of bastards, but we'll see to that one day, too.

And just to be on the safe side, he thought as he leaned back in his chair, he would send a few Federation men in to—ah—give assistance to the president of the STC. Maybe even send a ship to buzz over Central, strike a little fear into everyone, Citizen Altho Franken included. Let him know that Jonal Herrera expected him to keep his word.

Herrera nodded decisively and leaned forward.

After making a very brief 3-V call the Chairman quickly penned a memo to accompany the copies of Juliene's report. Those to whom he was sending copies would have to know the true gravity of the situation—he could accomplish nothing by lying to the men upon whom his life and power depended.

The Federation has suffered a defeat, he said in effect, serious but not fatal. The enemy has won this engagement but only with heavy losses. Now he must proceed to Earth to make good his claims of victory

—and Earth will be no easy conquest: she is heavily protected by Orbital Forts, the Lunar Garrison, the Auxiliary Terrestrial Defense Forces and the remnants of the armada that is even now rushing to her aid. In addition STC patrol ships are headed for Earth to assist in the home planet's defense. The Federation has lost a battle, he said, but not the war. We will not sue for peace. To make good his victory the enemy must take Earth herself, and—so said the Chairman— that he cannot do. His fleets will smash against the rock of the Federation and his rebellious challenge to law and order will thus be ended.

Chairman Herrera slipped his memo into the copier and leaned back in his chair. There were lines of fatigue in his face but anger burned brightly in his eyes. The rebels did not own Earth yet, and, by heaven, they would not do so as long as Jonal Herrera lived—for Jonal Herrera *owned* Earth and all the Federation—what there was left of it.

Chapter XVII

There were four living men and a girl in the large, plush office of the President of the Solar Trading Company. One of the men lay on the floor, bound, his eyes open and pleading, but unable to speak because of the gag in his mouth. Another sat behind the big desk, the grogginess of a stunner beam still on his face, but overlaid with an awakening anger. The two remaining men stood across the desk, weapons in their hands, and stared at him. The girl stood silently, unspeaking, watching and waiting. In a closet near the main office lay the body of an STC Pinker captain, dead from a slug of lead in his chest.

For a few moments after the brief battle Janas had feared that the sound of the gunshot would be heard and bring all the Pinkers in Central down on them, but apparently it was not so. Franken's office and the corridor outside were soundproofed; the acoustic insulation must have prevented the sound of the blast from being heard by anyone else in the building. For that Janas was grateful, though the necessity of killing an STC Pinker had left him with a sick and empty feeling.

"Sudden death is an occupational hazard of men in his line of work," D'Lugan said flatly.

"That doesn't make my being the instrument of it any more pleasant," Janas answered. "He was an STC man."

"That he was," D'Lugan agreed, but said no more.

While they waited for Franken to awaken D'Lugan brought Janas up to date on the events of the past few hours. As he had suspected there had been a spy in their midst, though even now Jarl Emmett was not sure of his identity. The unknown spy had relayed the events of the night before to Franken, who had then proceeded to have the conspirators arrested. A counterspy from Emmett's camp had learned of the coming arrests and alerted the Operations Supervisor. He had quickly taken steps to hold the vitally important Operations building and began alerting the other members of the conspiracy, telling them that one of D'Lugan's proposed plans was now in effect. Having been unable to contact Janas, Emmett had sent D'Lugan to warn him. Delayed, narrowly avoiding arrest himself, D'Lugan had arrived at Janas' suite just in time to assist him.

Modifying the plan slightly the next step was to get Janas, and together attempt to capture Altho Franken and his brother Bilthor and hold them until Jarl Emmett could come from Operations to take them.

"First we've got to revise corporate policy, right?" D'Lugan asked. "Okay, STC Central's computers, and particularly the Operation's computer, have to have Franken's policy of cooperation with the Federation removed and then replaced with strict neutrality. Well, that could be done in two ways. One is to get the Board of Directors to sign a countermanding order, but we'd never get them to do that. The other is to get an emergency priority order signed by the president and vice president in charge of Operations. That's what Jarl has in mind."

After a brief pause D'Lugan went on. "Franken here and his brother both have to sign and submit thumb and retinal prints to the computer before it will accept an emergency high level policy change. Once they do that Jarl can submit orders to the computer implementing the 'new' corporate policy."

"Do we have to take them to Operations to do that?" Janas asked. "Why can't we do it from here?"

"Well," D'Lugan said, "Jarl says that there are only half a dozen computer input stations in Central that will accept high level policy changes. All but one of them are in this building—but he doesn't think we stand much of a chance of getting to any of *them*. The remaining one is at Operations and Jarl still has control there. We'll have to take the Frankens there and feed in the information."

Franken finally pushed himself erect in his chair.

"What is this, Bob?" he asked.

Janas did not speak at once. After a long, empty silence he finally said: "You forced our hand, Al. We had to act."

"It's madness!" Franken spat. "What do you hope to accomplish? Tell me that."

"We hope to save your skin," D'Lugan answered, the stunner in his hand leveled at Franken, "and ours along with it."

"I'll see you shot," Franken replied. "You too, Bob. I don't give a damn how close a friend you've been. So help me, I'll see you shot."

"Maybe," Janas answered, "but maybe before then we'll be able to salvage something out of this mess."

"You're crazy, Bob," Franken cried. "The only way to save Earth is give the Federation what help we can."

"Save Earth!" Janas said. "Hell, Al, nothing can save Earth. Nothing in the universe can prevent the destruction of the Federation and the conquest of Earth. It's only a matter of time until Henri Kantralas sits in Geneva—if he doesn't blow it off the map. What we're trying to save is the STC."

"How?" Franken asked bitterly. "How do you knights-errant plan to save the STC?"

"Well," Paul D'Lugan said slowly in a terribly cold voice, "our first step is to get your brother Bilthor up here."

"And how are you going to do that?" Franken asked.

"You're going to call him," D'Lugan answered. With that he opened the butt of his stunner, made a slight adjustment with a pocket screwdriver, and closed the butt plate. "Citizen Franken," he went on slowly, "this isn't a regulation stunner. It's a special model carried by officers of the Rim Fleet. Maybe you recognize it. I've made an adjustment that increases the power several times. Now, if I were to fire it at you it would not merely temporarily paralyze your nervous system— it would destroy it. Do you understand me?"

Franken's face went ashen, but he did not reply.

"I said, do you understand me, Citizen Franken?"

Franken nodded at last.

"And I mean it."

Janas looked at the hard-faced young man and knew that he did mean it. A half centimeter movement of his index finger would reduce Altho Franken to a vegetable, would leave him no more than a pain-racked babbling idiot whose useless life could only be maintained by the most advanced techniques of Federation medicine.

"Citizen Franken," D'Lugan went on, "we have nothing to lose now. If you don't cooperate I shall certainly do it."

Franken looked at Janas, fear and pleading in his eyes.

"He means it, Al," Janas told him.

"And you'd let him?" Franken cried. "I thought you were my friend."

"I *was*," Janas said, "but Al, you just said you'd see *me* shot."

"I didn't mean it!" Franken yelled.

"He does," Janas replied. "And I won't stop him. I think you'd better call Bilthor."

"What about Enid?" Franken said suddenly with the desperate urgency of a man grasping at straws.

"What about her?" Janas asked, stiffening the grip on the .45 in his hand.

"You care a lot about her, don't you?" Franken

asked, color beginning to return to his cheeks, confidence to his voice. "You wouldn't want her hurt?"

"She won't be hurt," Janas said coldly.

"Are you sure?" Franken asked.

"What do you mean?" Janas felt anger rising in him.

"If anything happens to me . . ." Franken began.

"Do you claim you have her?"

"Yes," Franken answered. "My men captured her this morning."

"Where?"

"In her apartment."

"What apartment?"

"The one she has in Frisco, in the building where her brother lives."

"Prove it!" Janas felt his finger involuntarily contracting on the trigger.

"You'd better take my word for it, Bob," Franken said, something like a smile coming onto his face.

"You'd damn well better prove it, Al," Janas said. "Enid wasn't in her apartment this morning or any time today. She left it yesterday."

"Nobody saw . . ." Franken began, then realized his error. The smile vanished; the ghost of confidence went out of his face.

"Call Bilthor," Janas said, gesturing toward the communicator with his pistol.

Slowly, like a man weighted down on a high gravity planet, Franken moved his hand toward the communicator on his desk.

"Don't do anything stupid," D'Lugan said.

Franken nodded, and punched out a code on the communicator.

"Citizen Biltho Franken's office," came a pleasant female voice. From where he stood, Janas could not see the face in the tank. "May I help ... Oh, Citizen Franken."

"Connect me with Bilthor," Franken said, his voice shaken and cracked.

"He isn't in his office at the moment, sir," the girl said. "And I don't believe he is wearing his pager." There was a pause. "No, sir, he left it in his office. May I have him call you when he returns, Citizen Franken?"

Franken looked up at D'Lugan, then said. "Where is he?"

"I don't know, sir," the girl answered. "He didn't tell me where he was going. Should I have him call you, Citizen Franken?"

Franken looked up at D'Lugan. The other nodded slowly.

"Yes," Franken said. "Tell him it's important." Then he broke the connection.

"We'll wait," D'Lugan said.

"You can't," Franken protested. "I have appointments. People will wonder what's happened. What about Captain Tellzer?" He gestured toward the closet where the security officer's body lay. "The Pinkers will check."

"You'd better hope they don't," D'Lugan said, sitting down in a chair across the desk from Franken, the stunner never wavering from the other man's chest. "Call out front and tell them to cancel all your appointments this afternoon. And tell them that Tellzer went out the back way or something."

Under protest Franken complied.

"You'll never get away with it," he said, once he had completed the call.

D'Lugan glanced at his watch. "Jarl should be on his way here with a chopper now. He had a plan for getting away from Operations without being detected. If we could only get Bilthor up here we'd have a chance."

A smug expression had started to form on Franken's fleshy face when the communicator buzzed. Franken started, his face going white.

"Answer it!" D'Lugan snapped.

When Franken did not move at once D'Lugan stepped forward and waved the stunner in his face. Franken nodded abruptly and complied with the order. His right index finger stabbed a button on the communicator.

"Good afternoon, Al," said a voice from the speaker of the desk communicator. "Did you want me for something?"

After a moment's hesitation, Franken finally spoke. "Yes, I did. Will you come up to my office, please."

"I'm awfully busy, Al," replied Bilthor Franken's voice. "There's some kind of trouble over at the Operations building. I'm not sure what's going on. Couldn't you tell me about it over the 'com?"

"I need to see you in person," Franken said, staring at the barrel of D'Lugan's stunner.

"Is something wrong?" Bilthor asked.

"No, no," Franken said after a moment's pause. "I just need to see you."

"Okay," Bilthor sighed. "I'll be up in a couple of minutes. 'Bye." There was a click as he broke the connection, the puzzled sound of his last few words hanging in the air like fluorescent question marks.

Franken leaned back in his chair, glaring at D'Lugan and Janas. "He's coming."

"We know that," D'Lugan replied. "How will he come? Through those doors?" He gestured toward the huge double doors through which he, Janas and Maura had come.

"Yes," Franken answered.

"No, he won't," Maura said, breaking her silence for the first time. "There's a private entrance for vice presidents and board members."

"Where is it?" Janas asked.

"I'm not sure," Maura told him. "I only know they don't come through the regular way."

"How will he come?" Janas asked, turning to Franken.

"Are *you* threatening me, Bob?" the other asked slowly.

"You're damned right I am!"

Franken nodded sadly. "Go through that door on the right, back to the end of the corridor, and then left. There's a flight of stairs. He'll come that way."

"Thank you," Janas said coldly, then looked at D'Lugan.

"You stay here," D'Lugan suggested. "Keep him covered. I'll greet Citizen Bilthor."

When Janas did not reply at once, D'Lugan spoke again: "Look, captain, there's a lot more than just friendship involved here. It doesn't matter that this slob was your friend once. What happens to the STC is more important that he is."

Janas nodded grimly. "Don't worry, Paul," he said at last. "I'll do what I have to do."

D'Lugan shot him one of his brief, rare smiles, and turned to leave.

"Do you want to exchange weapons with me?" D'Lugan asked as he paused in the doorway. "We can set this stunner back on regular power."

"No," Janas replied, glancing down at the .45 in his hand. "I feel more comfortable with this one."

"Be careful, Paul," Maura said suddenly, her voice strained and thin.

"I will be," D'Lugan said softly, a gentleness to his voice and in his face that Janas had never expected to see.

Maura mouthed the words "I love you." D'Lugan nodded, something that might have been a sad smile on his lips, and then went through the doorway and down the corridor.

"Touching," Franken said sarcastically.

"Shut up!" Janas snapped, spinning to face him.

"There was a long period of silence before Franken spoke again, a strange calmness seeming to have settled over him once D'Lugan was out of the room.

"Why have you gotten mixed up in this, Bob?"

"I don't think you'd understand, Al," Janas said, sitting so that he could keep his eyes on Franken's hands. "And I don't think I could explain it to you."

"I'd like to know," Franken said, a sound like sincerity in his voice.

"Then let me tell you this," Janas said, wanting to try, at least, to explain his actions to this man whom he had called his friend for nearly a century. "I've spent most of my life Out There." He gestured skyward. "I've touched down on just about every world where men live and I've seen what people are doing. They're building a new civilization, Al, a hundred new civilizations. They've started from scratch on a thousand worlds and they're doing their damnedest to build the best things they can for themselves.

"It's not easy. Oh, Odin, Rama, Orpheus, maybe half a dozen others are—were—pretty well in hand, but as for the rest of them, they've just started clearing the land.

"And they've remembered a lot of things you people on Earth seem to have forgotten. Things that built the STC and the early Federation. They don't have security and they don't want it, not the kind the Federation gives. They've been pushed around by the Federation for centuries. They think they've been forced to give too much for too little in return. They won't take it any longer. And I think that maybe they're right, a lot of them."

Janas paused for a moment, looked out the window, glanced back at the girl who sat silently, her eyes on him.

"The Federation's finished, Al. Dead right now but doesn't know it. But so are the men who are ending it. There's a dark age coming. Anyone with two eyes and the will to see with them knows it, and there's nothing we can do to stop it. It's two hundred years too late.

"But maybe, just maybe, and that's the best we can hope for, maybe if we can keep the STC intact we can save something from the ruins.

"You know, Al, perhaps this is the most important thing, the STC. I'd think you'd understand that."

"Production and trade are what build civilisations, Al. The finest arts and sciences in the universe don't mean a damned thing if men can't exchange their ideas and their goods. That's how the STC built what we call the Federation, by trading goods and ideas, by letting men exchange on a free market, a market that the STC kept free by its strength. No government ever dared challenge it and those it traded with. That's freedom, Al.

"My father was an STC captain and so was his father before him. My family's been in the STC as far back as I can trace it. The STC's older than the Federation, Al. It made the Federation but it hasn't grown corrupt along with it. It couldn't and stay alive. It had to stay strong and independent, or it would have gone under.

"Maybe the STC is the most important thing in the universe. I believe in it. It's my *country* and I thought it was yours. And I damned well don't intend to see it destroyed because the Federation is sick and rotten and is collapsing in upon itself. I want the STC to survive and I'll do anything I have to do to see that it does."

A distant sound came through the thick paraglas window behind Franken's desk, the heavy droning of a helicopter moving through the afternoon air, coming from somewhere outside of Central toward the Graham Franken Building.

As Janas turned to look out, a sudden faint buzzing came from Franken's desk.

"What's that?" Janas asked.

"Facsimile machine," Franken answered. "Priority message."

Slowly Janas walked around the desk, stood behind Franken and watched a sheet of paper slide from a slot in the top of the large wooden desk. The first words he saw were: "Memo from the desk of Jonal Herrera, Chairman of the Terran Federation." Janas snatched the sheet of paper from the slot.

"What is it?" Franken asked.

Janas was silent for a moment, then spoke: "Proof that we're right. The expeditionary force met the rebels about seven and a half parsecs out. The rebels won. What's left of the Federation fleet is running for home as fast as it can."

Franken's mouth dropped open; for a moment he struggled for words.

"It's not decided yet," he stammered at last. "They don't have Earth!"

"Janas!" a voice yelled from a long way off, from down the corridor into which D'Lugan had gone.

Then Janas thought he heard another sound: the rasping of a power weapon.

Janas stood for a moment in indecision.

"It's all over for you, Bob," Franken said, a weak smile coming across his face. "Bilthor's no fool."

Chapter XVIII

Solar Trading Company patrol ship number 438 had lifted from the uneasy Rim world of Loki, taking with it almost the full garrison of STC Pinkers. Loki lay under a shaky truce, dominated by rebel victories in the Rim. The rebel commander who all but controlled the planet had refrained from acting against the STC base, waiting to see which way Altho Franken would jump during these, the last stages of the Great Rebellion. Fortunately for the STC garrison, Franken's decisions had not yet become known on the edge of the galaxy except by STC officials.

Aiming away from the blackness and dwindling stars of the Outer Rim, heading into the brightness of the Federation's Spiral Arm, PS 438 had jumped into Non-space and accelerated toward Earth, its commander halfway expecting to be followed by angry rebel warships.

At a prearranged spot PS 438 returned to normal

space, now deep in the bright ocean of stars. A rendezvous signal was beamed broadly into space and was soon answered by another such signal. PS 438 shortly grouped with three other STC patrol ships, and together the four small battle craft returned to Non-space.

One by one, at selected spots in normal space, carefully avoiding contact with forces of the Alliance, other patrol craft joined them. By the time PS 438 had crossed half the distance between Loki and Earth the flotilla numbered better than a dozen, and together they moved Earthward.

There should have been more ships, the commander of PS 438 told himself. He had read the orders that STC Central had sent out, several times over, and he knew exactly what was supposed to be happening. The Solar Trading Company was abandoning its millennium-long tradition of neutrality, now siding with the Federation. All STC patrol ships were to rendezvous near Saturn in the Solar System and then accept whatever commands Chairman Herrera gave them.

So the PS 438's commander had complied with his orders, though with some degree of reluctance. He was an Earthman by birth but had spent some twenty-five years in the Outer Rim. He had almost come to think of himself as a Rimmer; his wife was from Loki and his children had never seen Earth. He had thought of himself as a Rimmer until the orders had come from Central.

Then he told himself he was a Terran. Earth was his home, the home of all mankind, and it was his duty to defend her against the rebels. He told himself that, but he was not sure whether he really believed it.

He had waited until the last minute to give his men

their orders, but even at that a number of them had managed to vanish before their departure. Desertion was a criminal act, especially now that they were technically under the orders of the Federation, but he had sympathised with them, especially with those men to whom Earth was no more than a legend of the past and a tyrant of the present. Those *true* Rimmers, those outworlders who had never even seen Earth, how could you expect them to fight for Earth and the Federation against their own people?

So when PS 438 lifted from Loki and began her trip toward Earth her crew was short, and the Pinkers he carried with him were fewer than they should have been. But he understood.

He also understood when some of the patrol ships did not meet them at the prearranged spots. The commanders and crews of those ships had not been willing to join in *that* fight. It was a filthy, nasty thing, this war, and he coud blame no man for wanting to keep out of it.

Oh, God, he told himself, if only I had the courage to run.

He looked out into the darkness of normal space, at the bright stars that were even now sullied with the blood of men waging war against men, and he wondered if PS 296, which was supposed to meet them at that spot, would come. In a way he hoped that she would not.

Chapter XIX

Janas stood looking at the smirk that had spread across Altho Franken's face and he fully realized for the first time, realized to the core of his being, that this was a stranger, an enemy, a fool or a coward, but not his friend.

Leaping forward, Janas swung the heavy butt of his .45 automatic against the temple of the man who sat behind the desk. Franken tried to jump away to avoid the blow but Janas was faster still. The metal connected with a dull thud; Franken gasped, fell backward, tumbling out of the chair onto the thick carpet. Janas stood over him for an instant, breathing hard.

"Watch him," he snapped to the girl who had not moved during the action but now came to her feet. "If he wakes up, hit him again. Hard!"

Then he spun, running out of the room and into the corridor. He heard again the rasp of an energy weapon, a needle pistol, probably.

The corridor was a blur as he ran down it to its end, then to the left. He heard D'Lugan's deadly stunner, its generator screaming shrilly. Then he saw them. D'Lugan lay against the wall, smoke billowing around him as the carpet burned under him. There was blood on his face. His left leg was buckled under him, blood making a bright stain on the portions of the carpet that had not yet caught fire. The muscles of his face were pulled tight, baring his teeth in a hateful grin.

A man in the uniform of a Pinker lay on his face a meter or so from D'Lugan. Though there was no blood his posture spoke loudly of the fact that he was unable to move; he was dead or dead-in-life, for D'Lugan's stunner had brought him down.

Three men stood there: two were Pinkers, one aiming his needler toward the fallen D'Lugan, the other facing Janas, his weapon coming up; the third was a paunchy civilian, his ashen face bearing a strong resemblance to Altho Franken's.

Suddenly the tableau broke. Two Pinker needlers rasped almost simultaneously. Janas felt a vague stinging sensation in his left shoulder as he leaped to one side, acrid smoke billowing into the air.

The heavy .45 in his hand spoke. There was a tremendous roar in the confined space as the chemicals in the tiny metal chamber within the weapon exploded. A slug of metal, propelled by oxidizing chordite, spun down the weapon's barrel, out and across to the nearest of the startled Pinkers. His face collapsed inward; the back of his head exploded, scattering hair, bone and brains against the wall behind him. As if a hurricane wind had struck him, he lifted off the floor, back against the wall. Then the thing that had been a man fell to the floor and lay in a pool of its own blood.

A needle-thin beam of energy had leaped from the other Pinker's weapon, had found D'Lugan—and the angry young man who had survived the stupid blunders called the Battle of '77 died.

The .45 fired twice more, as rapidly as Janas' index finger could draw back the trigger. Two more metal slugs crossed the smoke filled air, and both found their target, the chest of the Pinker who had taken Paul D'Lugan's life. The first bullet shattered his left rib cage; he was all but dead when the second broke into his breastbone. His needler fired again as he stumbled back, the reflex of a dying animal, but its beam reached nothing but the ceiling.

Robert Janas felt sick for a moment; sick from the pain that had suddenly blossomed in his left shoulder, sick from the mingling odors of seared flesh, burning wool carpet, chordite fumes; sick from the death of a man who had, only minutes before, become his friend.

Bilthor Franken screamed, the hoarse, nightmare scream of a man who suddenly finds himself in a reality which he cannot accept. He turned to run down the stairs up which he had come. Janas' weapon fired for the fourth time, above Bilthor's head, blasting plaster from the wall of the staircase.

"Stop!" Janas yelled.

The other man halted, then slowly turned to face him.

"That way," Janas said, gesturing back down the hallway. "Go on. Now!"

Bilthor hesitated again. Janas brutally gestured with his weapon. The other man finally responded, half walking, half staggering.

Moments later Janas and his captive were back in Franken's plush office. The STC president had begun to stir, a painful daze on his face as he tried to rise from the floor.

Maura shot a questioning look at Janas, fear and sadness mingling behind her green eyes.

"He's dead," Janas softly told her, and turned away. He did not want to look at her face, at the pain that shattered her pretty features.

From outside the office, through the stillness that had suddenly come over it, Janas could still hear the roar of the approaching helicopter, louder now. Looking out through the broad windows he saw the aircraft waddling through the afternoon air, coded with the bright colors of the STC Operations Division.

"Maura," Janas snapped, "how do we get to the roof?"

The girl looked at him blankly. The words had failed to reach her, as though she did not know that he had spoken to her.

"The roof!" he said. "We've got to get there before anyone else comes."

The girl snapped out of her trance. "This way, I think," she said in a weak voice.

Janas grabbed Franken and roughly hauled him to his feet.

"Walk, damn you," he said. "Help him," he told Bilthor. "I don't want to have to kill either of you."

Bilthor, white fear on his face, crossed to his dazed brother and allowed him to throw his arm across his shoulder. Franken looked at Janas with pain and hatred in his eyes.

"A better man than either of you could ever be just died out there," Janas said with a voice he could barely keep under control, "and you'd damn well better make his death worthwhile, or so help me ..." His voice trailed off. "Follow her," he gestured toward Maura who stood pale and damp-eyed but ready to lead them.

With very little hesitation the girl started and the three men followed. Soon she found the escalator that led upward to the 'copter landing deck on the roof. The Franken brothers mounted the escalator with

Janas' gun at their backs, and a few minutes later they were out on the deck.

"Citizen Franken," a startled attendant said, seeing the blood on the president's face, "I thought I heard ..." Then he saw the weapon in Janas' hand and fell silent.

"Don't move," Janas said, and looked up to see the Operations chopper dropping down for a landing. He saw the pilot's face and waved grimly, ignoring the growing pain in his bleeding shoulder. Jarl Emmett was not a second too soon.

Chapter XX

The news leaked out, as bad news will do even under the tightest of security precautions: the armada had met the rebels and had been defeated; the rebels were headed for Earth to destroy the Federation.

*

It was already night at the Federation Lunar Garrison Outpost in Copernicus Crater. The line of darkness had spread down along the ring walls, into the depths of the crater, and gradually across to the opposite wall, slowly moving in its endless march around the tiny planet. The sky had not changed with the coming of night; it remained as pitch as ever, though Earth had grown slightly, ever so slightly, as Luna's face swung around toward her lighted side. Pale, bluish-green Earthlight gave the rugged landscape a surrealistic feeling that was not altogether unpleasant.

Such would have been Corporal Kaire Lee Chan's thoughts had they been verbalised. But Corporal Chan was not really thinking at that moment while he stood gazing up at the bright, slightly more than half-full Earth. He was not sure what he was doing other than walking his guard perimeter around the Copernicus Post in the age-old tradition of armies since the dawn of history.

There was something inside Corporal Chan that might have been fear, but that was not verbalised either. It lay deep within him, a cold lump of stone in the pit of his stomach that he could neither digest nor regurgitate. It was there, and he had grown rather used to it.

Still, though he had been in Federation uniform for quite some time, time enough to earn his corporal stripes, Chan could not think of himself as a soldier, and he really wasn't. He was a fairly competent hover-car mechanic and would always be just that, no more and no less, no matter what kind of uniform they put on him.

Corporal Chan looked longingly at the paraglas dome some kilometer and a half away, brightly lit, full of air and heat and beer and the half dozen or so girls that the Federation allotted to the soldiers who served in the old Copernicus Post. And Chan wanted to scratch his nose and smoke a cigarette, neither of which he could do inside his spacesuit—and he steadfastly refused to allow himself to think of the girls, all soft and warm and sexy and waiting to give a tired soldier just exactly what it was he wanted from a girl.

He knew better than to think of them while he was on guard duty.

He looked back up at the sky again, and the half-Earth, and remembered the rumor that was going around—the rumor that said that the rebs had beaten old Julie and were heading like hellbats for Earth. Chan didn't believe it. Not really. Old Julie was a hell of a soldier; he could beat *them*. But . . . something in his mind said maybe it's true. Kantralas is older and sharper than Julie, so they say. Maybe . . .

A cold chill went up his spine and he had a sudden vision of a sky filled with ships, bombs and missiles and energy beams raining down toward Luna's surface, blasting away the domes and tunnels and fields and . . . and Corporal Kaire Lee Chan.

Chan gripped his energy rifle a little tighter in his gauntleted hands and took one determined step after another around his perimeter.

*

In the city of Great Rio De Janeiro, in the near slums of the old Copacabana Beach area, a man who was suspected of being a sympathizer with the accursed rebels was dragged out of his home by a suddenly fearful, blindly enraged mob, a mob screaming for the blood of those who had threatened their homes and security, who had threatened the status quo that, good or bad, was life as they knew it.

The mob swelled as it marched down the new *Avenida Rio Brancho*, out toward the huge monolith called, in happier times, Sugar Loaf Mountain. There was the smell of blood in the air as the mob prodded the poor fisherman forward, their growing chant drumming in his ears, deafening him to all else: "Up the Federation! Up the Federation!"

He tried to join them in their chant, to show them that he wasn't what they thought he was, but a big, hairy Neanderthal of a man slapped him in the mouth when he opened it to yell.

A kangaroo court seemed to materialize out of nowhere in the center of the broad avenue, and there the noisy procession stopped, exhaling its stale collective breath, to watch the trial and execution of the traitor, Citizen Fontes Silva.

The trial, if it can be called by such a name, was mercifully short. In no more than fifteen minutes a jury of his neighbors, friends and peers had formed, had heard the prosecution—there was no defense; his wife attempted to present one, but she was carried away screaming—and had passed sentence: death by stoning. Now!

The poor, dazed, confused fisherman, whose gravest crime had been to doubt the godhood of Jonal Herrera, felt the first of the rough stones smack against his back, just below his shoulder blades, tearing the cloth and ripping his skin. He stumbled forward to meet a second stone, just below his left eye. Blinded and hurt, Fontes Silva fell to his knees. The third stone struck his groin, skillfully, brutally aimed. He screamed, tried to rise, but the fourth and fifth stones, one to his cheek, shattering teeth, and one to his chest, knocked him back. He counted no more stones after that—he only screamed and died.

*

Petrinja was one of several towns in the Balkans with that name. This one was probably the smallest, hardly more than a village, and technically a part of the Skopje Complex, though it was an independent town for all practical purposes. In Petrinja there was a magistrate who prided himself on his knowledge of interstellar affairs and his loyalty to the glorious Chairman, Jonal Herrera. This magistrate had a daughter whom he had unimaginatively named Katrina—and she, just as unimaginative as her father, had married a young man named Peter. Peter, however, was an outspoken admirer of rebel General Henri Kantralas, which brought no ease to the magistrate's household.

On the day the news of the Federation's defeat escaped from behind locked doors in Geneva the magistrate called a special meeting in the Petrinja town hall, and young Peter attended, with a long, sharp hunting knife tucked under his coat. As the old magistrate cursed and reviled the names of Kantralas and of the Alliance of Independent Worlds, young Peter leaped up onto the stage—and sank the knife into his father-in-law's heart.

*

Claude Smith-Henderson, titleless leader of the Brethren of Deliverance, upon hearing that the Battle of Armageddon had at last been fought, rejoiced at the imminent coming of his Savior Lord. Smith-Henderson, his long, graying beard blowing across his shoulder, quickly ran to tell his flock of the news.

After listening to a short sermon and joining in a brief prayer service, the Brethren and their wives abandoned their homes in the town of Big Bell, Perth Complex, Australia, and sought the higher lands to the west of Meekatharra.

As Smith-Henderson led them north and then west, out to where the Deliverer could more easily find them and distinguish them from the uncounted multitudes of unrighteous who populated the Earth, their burning homes filled the sky with a pillar of smoke by day, a pillar of fire by night.

When they at last reached their sanctuary, a high spot of ground covered with no more than yellow spring grass, Smith-Henderson erected an altar and knelt to pray. And then he and his flock waited for the world to end.

*

Smoke also billowed skyward in the Tientsin Complex of East Asia as a mob attacked the Federal Governor's mansion, smashing windows, screaming insults to the Chairman and his henchmen, raping the Governor's youngest daughters, setting fire to the building, and demanding that the Federation surrender before the rebel warships began bombing Earth.

The Governor had fled for his life in an official staff hovercar, leaving his two pretty daughters to the mercies of the mob. One of the girls, fifteen years old, survived to tell the story.

*

Citizeness Vivian Franz, a twenty-three year old model and sometimes 3-V actress, stopped in the middle of the ancient "Times Square" district of Manhattan, North Atlantic Complex. Her head was spinning with the frightful news she had just heard: the Federation fleet had been destroyed and the rebel general, that Henri Kantralas, had sworn to bomb Earth like the Federation had bombed Antigone.

In her mind she could see it: the ships coming down through the sky above the Manhattan skyline, great terrible blasts of flame wiping that ancient town away, boiling the East and Hudson Rivers, destroying everything that mattered to her. And what was there she could do about it?

Vivian stood beside a weathered statue of some ancient Chairman of the Federation—she didn't know his name—and laid her purse down on the grass plot that surrounded it.

There was nothing she could do, she told herself. In a few days, maybe even in a few hours, the rebels would be there and Vivian Franz would die—die!

She shook her head, trying to drive the idea away, but it would not leave her. It clung there, stark and awful in her mind, the rebel ships in the sky and Vivian dying as they destroyed Manhattan. And there was nothing she could do.

Suddenly she knew what she would do. If she were going to die then at least she was going to do *something* before she did, something wild and crazy, something to give a kind of insane meaning to the last hours of her life.

Foot traffic around her came to a halt to watch, though no one tried to stop her, not even the officers of the law, who did not seem to care, not any more.

First she carefully removed her shoes and set them beside the wall that surrounded the plot of grass under the statue. Then she removed her blouse, folded it neatly, and placed it on the sidewalk beside the shoes. Finally she took off her skirt and panties, folded them as well, and laid them on top of the blouse.

Standing stark naked under the imposing bulk of the age-spotted statue Vivian Franz took loose the hair that was piled high above her head and let the dark curls tumble down her back. After climbing over the low wall she sat down on the spot of turf, just wide enough to hold a human body stretched full length, and looked back at the people watching her.

"We're all going to die, you know," she said with a voice that surprised her with its calmness. "We don't have much time." She paused and looked into the eyes of the man standing nearest her. "If any of you want me," she said, "take off your clothes and come here."

She had more than a few acceptances before her strength gave out.

*

Walter Duncan carefully bolted the door and then proceeded to push as much furniture against it as his strength would allow. When he had finished he stood back for a moment to survey what he had done, whispering to himself, "That ought to do it."

"Walt?" Ledith, his term-wife, called from the landing at the top of the stairs, "What in heaven's name are you doing?"

Duncan pushed a thin strand of white hair out of his eyes and turned to look up at the little old woman that his wife, over the decades, had become.

"Just takin' a few precautions, that's all."

"Don't be a fool, Walt," Ledith called down. "Come up here and get to bed this minute."

"Be up shortly, dear," Duncan said, turning to the antique firearm that hung above the pseudo-fireplace. He took down the old weapon, worked its action and hoped that the shells would still fire. "Haven't used this damn' thing in better than fifty years, must be," he said to himself.

Tucking the rifle under his arm Duncan started up the stairs.

"Walt, what do you think you're going to do with *that*?" Ledith asked indignantly.

"Never you mind," Duncan replied cryptically as he went into the bedroom.

Crossing to the nearest window he pulled the curtains aside and looked out toward Alford, two kilometers or so away. There was just enough light left in the sky for him to make out the silhouettes of the town's buildings, spotted now with lights. The outskirts of Aberdeen Complex itself were too far away for him to see them, but he knew that Aberdeen would be one of the targets of those hell-born rebels. Well, Duncan told himself, if they did decide to attack Aberdeen, and if they did decide to come up the Don toward Alford, they'd find at least one man ready for them, by God!

Duncan smiled toward his wife, propped the old rifle beside the bed, and began to undress with the slow deliberation that comes with age.

Chapter XXI

Janas unceremoniously pushed Altho Franken and Bilthor into the hands of the men who leaned out of the helicopter. Behind him he heard shouts. One of the men in the helicopter's open hatch straightened up, an energy pistol in his hand, and fired a blast across Janas' shoulder. Shoving the .45 into the waistband of his trousers, the starship captain grabbed Maura around the waist with both hands and half threw her into the chopper. As soon as she had gained a foothold, he leaped upward behind her and into the craft.

He was motioned into the empty copilot's seat beside Jarl Emmett and strapped himself in as Emmett revved the engine and the machine lifted from the deck. While they rose there were shots aimed in their direction, but they ignored them.

"We got them," Janas said.

Emmett nodded, not looking away from his controls, and then asked: "Paul?"

"Dead," Janas said tonelessly, his voice sounding loud in the quiet, acoustically padded cabin.

An expression of pain briefly crossed Emmett's face. "He was a good man."

Janas nodded but did not speak. With great deliberation he withdrew the clip from the butt of his .45 and replaced the five shells he had expended. He then slipped the pistol back into his waistband, almost hoping that he would have the opportunity to use it again—he wanted *them* to pay for Paul D'Lugan's death, but who *they* were he was not sure.

One of the men from the rear of the 'copter came forward to ask Janas about his shoulder. When Janas replied that it was painful but not really serious, the man ripped open the scorched cloth of his shirt, swabbed away the blood, and sprayed on a temporary anesthetic bandage.

"We've got twenty, maybe thirty minutes," Emmett said. "If we can't get the orders changed and Luna notified by then we've lost."

Janas looked at him. "What do you mean? The Pinkers won't do anything drastic as long as we have *them.*" He tilted his head back to indicate the Franken brothers.

"No," Emmett said, "if it were only the Pinkers we could hold out for several days. Operations is virtually impregnable, short of nuclear weapons that is. It was built to withstand a crashing spaceship and it would probably take a pretty good size nuke to do much damage."

"The Federation?" Janas asked.

Emmett nodded coldly. "As soon as they get wind of what we're doing they'll send everything they've got to stop us—and that'll include hydrogen bombs."

Janas sat back in the seat. Then we aren't home free, he thought.

"When you were on Earth the last time," Emmett said as he raised the helicopter high above the buildings of STC Central and turned the craft out toward the huge, lonely building that housed the heart of the Solar Trading Company Operations Division, "ten years ago, and you told me what things were like Out There, I never imagined that it would end like this."

"No," Janas said, shaking his head, "I didn't either. I don't know whether I would have started it if I had known."

"You would have," Emmett said. "We're doing what we have to do."

"What about Miriam?" Janas asked.

"Safe," Emmett answered. "I sent her to the lodge this morning. Not many people know where it is. This'll all be over before they can find her."

Silently Janas hoped that the same were true of Enid. He was sure that Franken's men had not been able to find her. Franken's bluff would have had more substance had he really known where she was. But what about the Federation, he asked himself. They're not amateurs at this like Altho. With all the power and wealth of the Federation behind them it would only be a matter of time until Herrera's agents found her—if they were looking for her. But, and this was Janas' hope, as Emmett had said, perhaps it would all be over before then—twenty or thirty minutes. Then it wouldn't matter if they found Enid. They could not use her against Robert Janas, for then, win or lose, he would be dead or captive and the STC would have been saved or lost. Oh God, Enid, he cried to himself, I didn't want you mixed up in this.

Three armed helicopters, marked with the code colors of the STC Pinkers, part of a larger group that hovered in the air above the huge Operations building, rose higher into the air, swinging up to intercept Emmett's chopper.

"Well," Emmett said, "we have a reception committee waiting for us. I wonder what took them so long."

The helicopter's radio burst to sudden life as the Pinker's siren broke in. Janas' hand grasped toward the volume control to cut back the screaming.

"Identify yourselves," a strident voice said via radio as the siren abruptly ceased. "This is Lieutenant Hallbern, STC Pinkers. I demand that you identify yourselves." With that a rocket burst from the nearest of the Pinker 'copters roared past the Operations craft, missing it by no more than a few meters.

"They didn't mean to hit us with *that* one," Emmett said.

"Shall we contact him?" Janas asked.

Nodding, Emmett pointed out the small 3-V communications tank located in the center of the broad control panel.

"Lieutenant," Janas said into the microphone portion of the 3-V unit, "this is STC Operations Division helicopter—" he searched for an identification number "—number 545. Will you please switch to visual communications."

The Pinker officer did not speak but the receiving light above the 'copter's 3-V tank came to life. Janas adjusted the controls, brought into focus a grim face above a Pinker combat uniform.

"Lieutenant," Janas continued, "we have STC President Altho Franken and Vice President Bilthor Franken on board." Then Janas yelled back across his shoulder: "Bring 'em up so that he can see them."

The Franken brothers were roughly forced to the front of the chopper where their faces could be seen by the Pinker lieutenant.

"Any action you take against us will also affect them," Janas said when the Frankens had been taken back. "I suggest that you leave us alone."

The approaching Pinker helicopters slowed.

"We're going to land on the Operations building roof," Janas told him. "Their lives are in your hands, lieutenant."

"If they're hurt in any way . . ." the lieutenant said as the helicopters veered away. "Go on, dammit!"

The helicopter surged forward, past the point where the Pinkers would have intercepted it, and then swung down toward the roof deck of the ancient Operations building. As they came in Janas could see a dozen or so armed men on the roof, dressed in the work tans of Operations Division. There were two or three limp bodies, and here and there the roof deck was scarred and smoldering from recent energy blasts.

"They've held out," Emmett said as the 'copter's skids touched the deck.

Moments later, the huge blades still spinning, Emmett, Janas and the men who had been in the helicopter hustled the Franken brothers out and across the roof deck toward the elevators. Maura followed, blank faced, silent; brooding within herself.

"Jarl," a woman's voice called.

Janas turned to see Syble Dian, dressed in the tan coveralls of an Operations worker, an energy rifle tucked under her arm.

"Syble!" Emmett said. "What in the world are you doing?"

"Good afternoon, captain," she said to Janas as she came up to them. Then she looked at Emmett and shrugged. "Well, the legal department's not much use to us now, so I joined the 'illegal' department. I'm pretty good with a rifle, you know."

"I imagine you are," Emmett said, "but for God's sake, be careful. You could get yourself killed up here."

"So could those other fellows," she said seriously, gesturing toward the men who stood around the roof deck, armed and waiting for the Pinker helicopters. "Anyway, Hal put me in charge up here."

"You in charge?" Emmett asked. "I asked him to stay up here."

"He said he had something else he had to do," Syble told him. "He seemed quite anxious about it."

"Okay," Emmett said. "Be careful anyway."

"I will," Syble said slowly. "And you, Citizen Franken," she said to Altho, "you be careful too. Don't do anything foolish like *not* signing those papers."

Franken glared back at her, his lips a thin line cutting across his face.

"We'd better get on down," Emmett said, gesturing toward the open doors of the grav-elevator.

A few moments later they had entered the cramped elevator car. There was room enough for only five: Emmett, Janas, Maura and the two Franken brothers. As the doors closed behind them, Emmett glanced at his watch.

"How long?" Janas asked.

"Fifteen minutes, twenty at the most," Emmett said stiffly. "Everything's ready below. All they've got to do is to sign the orders, get thumb and retinal prints, and we can shove the orders into the computer. I already have tapes prepared with detailed orders for message capsules. We can get them off as soon as the computer accepts the policy changes. I've alerted Luna that orders will be coming through soon."

"Will Luna accept your orders?" Janas asked.

"I hope so," Emmett said. "I don't think that anyone's informed them that I'm no longer Operations Supervisor. We'll find out soon enough."

"You don't expect me to sign those orders do you?" Franken asked bitterly.

"You'll sign them if you want to live, Altho," Emmett said. "And I can't decide that for you. But let me tell you this; if I don't kill you myself, Federation bombs will. Now you decide."

Precious seconds rushed by as the elevator dropped them down toward the surface and below, down into the sub-basements of the huge, ancient Operations building, down toward the computer vaults and the machine that organized and supervised the operations of the vast starfleets of the Solar Trading Company.

Janas had turned, about to add a comment to strengthen Emmett's words, when the compartment was plunged into darkness.

"What!" Emmett cried loudly as Maura stifled a scream.

Janas recognized the feeling at once—free fall. Power had failed in the Operations building, or at least in the elevator shaft, and with it the Contra-grav unit that raised and lowered the small car. The compartment in which they rode was plunging toward the bottom of the well, 980 cm/sec^2.

"Friction locks," Emmett said, "why don't they stop us?"

The mechanically operated friction locks that should have snapped from the sides of the car, grabbed into the walls of the shaft, and lowered the car slowly to the next exit were not operating. The car was not being slowed in its plunge down the long tube into the Earth, meter after meter into the rock that underlay the Operations building.

"Jammed," Janas said. "Somebody's trying to kill us."

That was the last thing Janas said before they hit bottom.

The fall ended with terrible swiftness—the floor rushed up to meet him, smashing against his feet, his knees, his whole body. Blackness became a blaze of light, filling the entire universe. Then blackness again.

Chapter XXII

The first matinée at Eddie's had just begun. There was a reasonably full house for that time of day when the curtains went up, exposing the simulation of the Odinese Craterlands and the twelve almost naked dancing girls who preceded the headline act.

The girls had almost finished their routine and the hidden band was ready to swing into its introduction music for Rinni and Gray, The Moondog Dancers, when the Federation soldiers, dressed in harsh combat green and not even bothering to display warrants, marched into the lounge. Neither the band under the floor nor the girls on the stage or even the couple who stood in the wings awaiting their musical cue were aware of the entry of the armed soldiers. Only a few of Eddie's patrons noticed them, and they, gradually becoming accustomed to seeing armed soldiers and even stranger sights in their city, quickly turned their attention back to the performance.

The soldiers stood in the shadows near the entrance as if waiting for some signal to tell them to do what they had come to do. Their leader, a young, downy-cheeked lieutenant, looked nervously about, his right hand continually flitting to and away from the service needle pistol on his hip. After a few awkward moments he pulled a cigarette from his uniform blouse pocket, clumsily placed it between his lips, and applied his lighter to its tip with shaking fingers. A private standing near him gave his superior officer a sidelong sneering glance, and then returned his eyes to the twelve beauties cavorting on the stage. He gave the lieutenant very little thought after that.

The lieutenant, for his own part, wished that he could allow his attention to be completely absorbed by the attractive girls; tried to visualise himself with the little brunette, third from the left. But it did not work. Too much of his mind was occupied with the two pieces of paper in his pocket beside the cigarettes and with what he had come there to do.

The drums of the hidden band rumbled, the horns squealed, and the chorus girls retreated toward the rear of the stage. A subdued chatter gave way to silence as a mournful guitar cued the headliners and heralded the pseudo-Moondog theme.

Light shifted from white to azure. Rinni—part running, part dancing, part floating, spreading a dissipating cloud of shimmering white fog behind her—came onto the stage, dressed only in the vanishing mists and the pale blue, decorated breechcloth. An involuntary gasp, a sigh, came up from the audience, or at least from the masculine half of it.

Behind her, in half serious, half light-hearted pursuit, came her lover-partner. What response he elicited from the audience was not audible, but the young lieutenant saw a desiring look on the face of at least one woman near him.

The pale-skinned, soft-cheeked, shaky-fingered lieutenant of the Federation Army dropped his cigarette to the floor, crushed it under the heel of his regulation boot, and hesitantly drew his needler from its holster.

"Let's go," he said in a tremulous voice—and his soldiers, no more veterans than he, tremulously followed.

With as much boldness as he could muster the young officer marched straight across the floor, ignoring as best he could the outraged gasps of the people against whom he rudely, nervously brushed. He brought his soldiers to within a few meters of the stage, halted, and took the two official forms from his breast pocket. Transferring them to his left hand he rested his right on the butt of his needler.

"Citizeness Rinni Kalendar and Citizen Grayson Manse," he said in a voice unnaturally high and thin, "by orders of the Chairman of the Terran Federation, pursuant to legislation passed this day by the Parliament of the Terran Federation, you are hereby charged with treason and placed under arrest pending trial by a military court of justice." It was a long speech and he was surprised to get through it as easily as he did. He looked back at the stage.

The two dancers had stopped suddenly, spun to face the source of the voice, anger and astonishment on their faces. Any words that they might have spoken were drowned by the gasps and cries of amazement from the watchers.

"Please come . . ." the lieutenant began, but his words were cut off by the leaping form of Gray, plunging off the stage toward the young officer.

"Run!" Gray yelled as he jumped.

Rinni's eyes followed him for a moment, wide and bright, pain and fear rippling across her delicate features. Then she turned.

Gray's plunge from the bright light of the stage into the darkness was miscalculated. He missed the lieutenant by a full meter, slamming against a portly man and the table at which he sat. The man sputtered indignantly and an energy rifle discharged, more by accident than intent, though the aim was excellent. Lightning leaped across the marble-topped table, spraying across Gray's naked chest, shoulders and face. He was not even able to scream before he died, faceless and smoldering.

The girl had crossed the stage and nearly escaped when the lieutenant recovered sufficient presence of mind to yell "Stop!" and at the same time, the result of months of intensive training, automatically fired the needle pistol that had somehow come into his hand. The training had down its work well.

The narrow tenth-level beam from the energy pistol seared across Rinni's hip, crisping flesh, burning away part of her breechcloth. She staggered forward, grasping blindly in front of her for something to catch her fall. The lieutenant's needler fired again, blackening a three centimeter circle between her shoulder blades.

Rinni gasped through burning lungs, half fell backward, and did a stumbling turn. Blood mingled with the redness of her lips, stark against the sudden whiteness of her face, as she staggered toward the front of the stage. The fragments of her scorched breechcloth fell away and she stumbled on naked, beautiful, dying.

"It doesn't matter," she cried. "It doesn't matter. You can't stop them from coming."

Then she fell forward across the stage.

She was dead when the doctor arrived.

*

In the San Mateo district of the San Francisco-Oakland Complex an auburn-haired girl stood at the window of an apartment high in the old building that overlooked San Francisco Bay. She gazed eastward across the water, over to the cluster of buildings that lined the man-made shore of New Mount Eden. She awkwardly fumbled with a cigarette, breaking it in the process of getting it out of the pack. Throwing it to the floor she more slowly, more carefully, concentrating all her attention on the act, withdrew a second and successfully transferred it to her mouth. It took her a while longer to find matches, and when she did it took her three tries to get one burning.

Exhaling a lungful of smoke, Enid Campbell looked directly down toward the surface some fifteen stories below her. She could not see the man whom she was sure was still standing in the shadows across the street from the apartment building, but she knew he was there; he had been there all day.

Who is he? she asked herself. And why? But she was not sure she really wanted to know the answer.

At last she turned away from the window, opaquing it, and stood for a moment deliberating. Then she went into the bedroom and began to remove her street clothes, carefully hanging them in the closet. Naked, she turned to the full-length mirror on the back of the door and stood looking at herself for a long while, the forgotten cigarette smoldering between her fingers. She felt within the attractive body she saw reflected in the mirror a pain and a hunger, an emptiness and a desire, and wanted Robert Janas with her so badly she could almost cry. Then, with a sudden, almost angry motion, she grabbed a peignoir from the closet, loosely draped it across her shoulders and returned to the apartment's living room.

She stopped in front of the 3-V unit sitting on a low table in the corner. It took all her will power not to punch out the code for a certain room in the STC Officer's Hostel in Central. She knew better than to call Bob. It could be very dangerous for them both. But that did not diminish her desire to do so.

She dropped onto a couch, the peignoir slipping off her shoulders, and lit another cigarette and wondered about her brother. He had not been in his apartment the morning before when she and Bob returned. In fact she had been unable to locate either him or his friends whom she had tried to call. But she knew where he was, she knew it as well as if he had told her himself—but she wanted to think it wasn't so; she wanted to believe that her hotheaded brother had not taken a stratoflyer to Geneva, a gun in his hand, to kill the Chairman. But she knew it was so. Oh, Rod, she cried to herself, oh, you fool!

Rising, her thin garment falling forgotten to the floor, Enid went back to the window, unpolarized it, and looked out at the bay and wished that the long, long day would end, and yet dreaded the coming of night.

Approximately nine thousand, six hundred and eighty odd kilometers east of the San Francisco-Oakland Complex, on the edge of the Rhone River, stood the ancient city of Geneva. In the center of an almost equally ancient park, once called *Place Neuve*, stood a complex of buildings which bore some slight resemblance to, though much larger than, the old Palace of the League of Nations that had stood near that spot some fifteen hundred years before.

It was night in Geneva, nearly 23:00, though that little deterred the constant stream of traffic that passed through this capital city of the Terran Federation, nor did it deter the Chairman of the Federation from calling an emergency night session of the Parliament to rubber-stamp another of his decrees. Grumbling and disaffected with "his majesty," the representatives of the Complexes of Earth and of her stellar colonies filed into the chamber and sat down to await the coming of *his* august personage.

Outside the building, still some half a kilometer from the Parliament chambers, six young men walked slowly down the tree-bordered lane that led to the Parliament building. They had been told that Jonal Constantine Herrera would soon make his appearance, would soon address the joint meeting of Parliament, and they meant to be there. Their object was to kill him.

The six young men, the action squad of the Sons of Liberty, all carried illegal needle pistols hidden inside their garish clothing, but for one of them the pistol seemed to weigh a thousand kilograms, for his was the weapon designated to bring an end to the life of the despot who ruled the crumbling Federation. He had volunteered to do it and now there was no way that he could back out of it. Like it or not, history was sitting in the palms of his sweaty hands.

Rod Campbell licked his lips with a dry tongue, glanced at the guards who stood beside the doors at the top of the flight of marble stairs that they approached, the main entrance into the Federal Parliament Chambers. His back muscles involuntarily tensed, almost painfully, and his empty stomach unpleasantly churned within him.

"Where do you think you're going?" the nearest of the guards asked as they mounted the flight of stairs.

"I don't know," Campbell stammered. "Just looking around, I guess." His casualness was a terribly thin veneer over the stark fear that grew cancer-like within him.

"Not here you ain't," the guard said. "Not tonight. Go some place else." He dismissed them with a wave of his hand.

Campbell reached up to scratch his head—and on that signal five needlers were ripped out into the open, five firing studs were depressed, five beams of energy bore toward the three uniformed guards. All three Federal guards died before gaining their weapons.

Drawing his own pistol, Campbell leaped toward

the doors, kicking them apart, and then jumped into the huge Parliament Chambers amid the clanging and screaming of alarms.

Rod Campbell never saw the Chairman.

Closed circuit 3-V monitors trained on the doors, wary for uninvited visitors, saw the events outside, saw Campbell kick open the doors and leap in. An operator sitting in a room high above the chambers then moved his hand to a toggle switch that activated two energy rifles trained on the doorway.

A sheet of flame came into being, for an instant outlining Campbell's figure, a dark humanoid form amid the white-hot glow of hell. Then that figure ceased to exist, became vapor and ash and charred bones blown back by the explosion of the melting energy pistol. The five young would-be assassins behind Campbell died as well, though not as quickly or painlessly.

Chapter XXIII

At first Janas could not remember where he was or how he had gotten there or why there was pain in his ankles and his left shoulder. Then the blackness began to recede a little from him, the blackness that was in his mind, and he opened his eyes and still saw darkness, though this was the darkness of the absence of light, and not the darkness of unconsciousness.

Shifting himself around enough to relieve the pain in

his ankles, he began to feel about. On his right he found something soft and warm that responded to his touch with a faint moan.

"Maura?" he asked.

"Captain," the girl replied in the darkness.

"Are you hurt?"

"No, I don't think so," the girl answered. "Are you?"

"Twisted my ankles, I think," he said. "Not serious."

"Bob," a voice said from his left, "it's me, Jarl. They didn't quite make it, did they?"

"Not yet," Janas answered. "I doubt that they expected to, at least not this way. Are you hurt?"

"Bumped my head. Other than that, okay. But if it hadn't been for the buffers at the bottom of the shaft we would have been killed."

"Altho?" Janas asked. "Bilthor?"

Altho Franken grunted reply, then said, "Bilthor's unconscious."

"He'll be okay," Janas said. "We didn't hit hard enough to break any bones. Now listen carefully, Al. Someone's trying to stop us from getting revised corporate policy orders out. At this stage I assume it's Herrera's men."

"This isn't my doing," Franken said gloomily.

"I believe you," Janas told him. "These people mean to stop us, Al, even if they have to kill you in the process. You remember that."

By this time Emmett had risen to his feet in the darkness and was trying to open the doors of the elevator car.

"I think we can get these doors open if you'll help me, Bob," he said.

"Wait," Janas told him.

"Why?"

"Whoever's doing this is probably outside there now," Janas said, "waiting for us to come out. We can expect them to be armed and we've only got one gun between us."

"We can't just sit here," Emmett said. "We don't have that much time."

"Your people ought to know what's happened by now and be on their way down here," Janas said.

"Yes, but still ... Emmett began but was interrupted by a banging on the car's door.

"Jarl?" a muffled voice came through the metal.

"Who is it?" Emmett asked.

"Hal Danswer," the voice replied. "What happened?"

Janas thought he heard Franken sigh with relief.

"Something happened to the power and the friction stops didn't work," Emmett answered. "Get us out of here."

"Just a minute."

Stepping to Emmett's side Janas whispered into his ear: "Stand away from the door."

"Why?" Emmett asked.

"Don't take any chances."

"With Hal? Hell, Bob, he's as trustworthy as you are."

"Do you know who the spy is?" Janas asked.

"No. It could be anyone."

"That's what I mean. Stand away from the door."

"You don't have to worry about Danser," Franken said lightly from the darkness.

"What do you mean?" Emmett snapped.

"Danser isn't trying to kill *me*," Franken said. "You see, he's working for me. He has been all along. How do you think I knew what you were planning?"

Emmett released something halfway between a curse and a groan, and Janas heard him move toward Franken.

"Hold it, Jarl," he said. "We'll take care of Al later. Right now you get out of the way."

While Emmett moved back into the compartment, pressing himself against the wall, Janas drew the .45 from his waistband. He leaned against the door frame, relieving as much weight as he could from his painful ankles, and waited. He did not have long.

Already there were the sounds of a metal tool being wedged into the tiny space where the two metal doors came together. The edge of the tool worked its way in, separated the doors slightly, and allowed a thin beam of light to fall into the dark car. Janas could see nothing save the tip of the tool wedged between the slabs of metal.

"We'll have you out in a shake," Hal Danser's voice said as another tool was placed into the crack. "Now, all together," Danser's voice went on. "On the count of three, pry. One. Two. Three."

There was a grumbling sound from the skewed doors as they began to slide apart, as hands gripped them and tore them open. Light spilled into the darkness.

For a moment Janas was partially blinded, but not enough that he could not distinguish the shapes of the three men, and the things that they held in their hands. He squeezed the trigger of his .45.

The men outside apparently had not expected the ones within the elevator car to resist, or to resist with such fury. The nearest of them stumbled backward, losing the grip on the energy weapon he carried, throwing his left hand up to stop the blood that suddenly gushed from the rip in the flesh of his right arm.

"Drop it, Janas!" Hal Danser commanded, bringing his needle pistol around toward the starship captain. "Get Franken," he yelled to the other man.

Janas fired twice more in quick succession. The first slug missed Danser and ended its flight somewhere down the long corridor behind him. The second was better aimed. Danser stumbled backward as it struck a heavy blow in his midsection, the activated beam of his needler cutting a great arc through the air, leaving behind it a trail of scorched metal and ionized air.

The third man had taken aim on Altho Franken and had already fired into the interior of the elevator car when Janas brought the automatic around to him. The beam of energy narrowly missed Franken, who had leaped to one side.

The .45's aim was bad; too low to kill but high enough to blow off the attacker's left knee cap and send him staggering backward, collapsing in pain. Janas fired again, this time directly into the other's face. The man died as he hit the floor.

Hardly pausing long enough to catch his breath, Janas turned back to the interior of the elevator car.

"Everybody okay?" he asked.

"I guess so," Emmett said. "Bilthor's awake." He gestured toward the dazed elder Franken.

"Maura?" Janas asked.

"Yes," the girl answered, her voice weak and uncertain.

"Herrera didn't order that," Franken said in a shaken voice. "He wouldn't have us *killed*."

"You really don't know what kind of man you're

dealing with, do you, Al?" Janas said. Turning back to Emmett: "We'd better get out of here."

"Can you walk?" Emmett asked.

"Yes." Gesturing toward the Franken brothers, Janas said, "Get out!"

As the president and vice president of the STC walked out of the elevator car half a dozen men came running down the corridor toward them, led by Juan Kai.

"Jarl, what happened?" Kai cried.

Emmett gestured toward Hal Danser.

"We had a spy, Juan," Emmett said coldly. "He tried to kill us. On *Herrera's* orders!"

Janas half dragged, half led Altho Franken across the large computer chamber to a big, paper-obscured desk that Emmett had indicated. Bilthor Franken followed, still dazed, an energy rifle prodding him forward.

Glancing at Janas, Emmett gestured toward a complex of screens and tanks against one wall. "We've jury-rigged radar and 3-V scanners," he said. "We can see what's going on topside."

In the nearest of the 3-V tanks Janas saw a panoramic view of the roof deck of the Operations building. There were even more armed men there than before and all of them were looking upward. In the clear blue sky Janas saw perhaps half a dozen Pinker helicopters, and beyond them, no more than a tiny speck, was the distant shape of a starship. Though faint and far away, he recognized the lines of a Federation warship.

"Your estimate was high, Jarl," Janas said in a hollow voice. "It didn't take the Federation as long as you expected."

Emmett froze. "Oh, my God," he said weakly.

Chapter XXIV

The grayness of Non-space was behind them and the glowing disk of ancient Sol was before them. The TSFF *Shilo* came down toward the plane of the ecliptic and aimed toward the double world of Terra-Luna, toward the blue-green planet and its white companion.

By now they were within radio range of Earth, though there was still some delay in communications between the ship and the home world. As the remnants of the fleet fell Earthward, the light-speed gap narrowed—too slowly.

Grand Admiral Abli Juliene had given orders to the communications crew: Report to Earth everything we know.

And that report, after giving Federation losses and estimated rebel strength in great detail, concluded with: shortly after breaking back into normal space, the Federation fleet had recorded information indicating that the rebels had broached normal space not far behind them and were even then but a few light-minutes farther from Earth. There would be no time for the Federation ships to land on Luna to refuel and refit. Please, concluded the admiral's report, advise us of our present orders. Where do we make our stand?

Something close to pandemonium broke out in the Federation headquarters in Geneva. It was happening too quickly, too soon. The experts had underestimated the enemy's strength, his will to win.

A few men in Geneva kept their heads. Among them were the officers of the Terran Federation Military Forces General Staff, who even then were issuing their orders for the final defense of Earth. Orbital Forts were put on full alert. The Lunar Garrison was ordered into space and into orbit around Earth, forming a hard line of defense at one hundred thousand kilometers, bulking their forces in the anticipated direction of rebel approach. The surviving ships of the F.E.F. were ordered to join with the Lunar Garrison forces and Admiral Juliene was placed in command. The Auxiliary Terrestrial Defense Force would be kept in reserve, under the personal command of the Chief of Staff himself. Solar Trading Company patrol ships within the Solar System were to be led by their own commander as a separate detachment under the overall command of Admiral Juliene. The out-system ships of the STC, already reported to be within a few light-days of Sol, would act on their own initiative, maintain liaison with the Chief of Staff. So Earth prepared to meet her attackers.

There was another man in Geneva who kept his self-composure, and that was Citizen Jonal Constantine Herrera, Chairman of the Terran Federation, who was ordering the preparation of his private cruiser. Have it fitted, fueled and waiting, he commanded. He was not a big enough fool to stay in Geneva if the rebels showed indications of winning. His death would

accomplish nothing, nothing at all, and his escape ...
Well, "he who fights and runs away ..."

There was a distant and little known planet that he
had long since prepared for such an event, though he
had never really expected to use it. Nevertheless it
was ready, a pleasant enough place fully equipped to
sustain Chairman Herrera, his staff, his friends, and his
harem for the rest of his natural life; to sustain him at
the level of luxury to which he was accustomed, and
it was far enough away so that he could probably
enjoy that luxury in safety.

Chapter XXV

Deep within the computer chambers below
the STC Operations building the president of the
Solar Trading Company suddenly laughed.

"Citizen Emmett, Captain Janas," he said slowly,
his words riding on his bitter laughter, "don't you
think you'd better surrender while you have the
chance?"

Something exploded inside Robert Janas. He spun
toward the man who had once been his friend, that
man's face blotted out by the rising red tide of anger.
Janas' right hand shot out, clenched in the hard knot
of a fist, and struck toward Altho Franken. There was
a thud, a snapping sound, a groan of agony, and
Altho Franken staggered backward, his eyes glazing,
his mouth and jaw twisted into an unlikely shape. He
collapsed, a clumsy bag of bones, to the floor.

Janas looked down at his hand. The skin over his knuckles was split and bleeding, but he smiled a bitter, angry smile.

"I think you broke his jaw," Jarl Emmett said tonelessly, the ghost of a smile playing across his lips.

"You'd better get a medic," Janas answered. "We need him awake so he can sign those orders."

Emmett glanced at the 3-V that displayed the sky above the building. "There's a warship out there, Bob."

"We may still have time," Janas snapped, bending to the limp form of Altho Franken and roughly lifting him to his feet. "We can keep trying till they blow us off the face of the Earth. Get a medic!"

While Emmett ordered that one of the Operations staff doctors come to the computer chambers at once, Janas propped Franken up in a chair, then turned to his brother, the vice president in charge of Operations.

"Sign that order," Janas said softly.

Bilthor looked at him, his eyes large and wide with fear.

"I said, sign that order!" Janas yelled.

Bilthor stepped forward, picked up the pen and slowly wrote his name at the indicated spot. He then stepped back, sought a chair as if in a fog, and collapsed into it.

More quickly than Janas had expected, Emmett found a doctor. The medic took one look at Franken, then glanced at Janas, questions on his face.

"Get him awake," Janas said.

The doctor did not speak, but opened his case, took out a spray hypo and pressed it against Franken's neck. There was a sudden hiss, then silence.

"Give him thirty seconds or so," the doctor said.

"This ought to keep him going for a few minutes, but not long."

"We don't need him for very long," Janas said.

He looked back at the 3-V tank. The Federation warship had grown in size until it was no longer possible for anyone to fail to recognize it for what it was.

"Jarl," Juan Kai, who had gone to the communications equipment, called from across the room.

"What is it?" Emmett yelled back.

"That warship's radioing us," Kai answered. "Do you want to answer?"

"Yes," Emmett snapped.

"What do you want me to say?"

"Ask them want they want." Emmett smiled briefly, ironically.

Franken had begun to stir. His eyes fluttered open and he looked up. He tried to speak but seemed to find that his jaw would not obey his brain.

"You can't talk," Janas said, "but you can listen. If you don't sign that order now, this minute, I'm going to kill you."

He leveled the .45 at Franken's eyes and snapped off the safety.

Franken's eyes sought his brother. Bilthor looked back at him, his face white, deflated, and he nodded. "Sign it, Al. For God's sake sign it, or they'll kill us all."

Franken peered at Janas, a strange, unfamiliar expression in his eyes.

"Think whatever you like," Janas said, advancing the pistol, "but by all that I love I'll blow your brains out myself if you don't sign that paper in thirty seconds."

Kai had made contact with the Federation warship

that now hung less than a kilometer above the Operations building. He channeled its commander's words into the speakers that ringed the communications chamber:

". . . at once. I am authorized by the Chairman to use thermonuclear weapons if you do not comply. You have exactly one minute to acknowledge or I shall do as I am authorized. I repeat . . ."

"Sign it," Janas said coldly.

Altho Franken reached for the offered pen, took it in a shaking hand, and carefully wrote his name above his brother's on the emergency priority corporate policy modification orders.

Jerking him to his feet, Janas half carried him to the computer recognition booth. He shoved Franken's face into a hood where a scanning device recorded the patterns of his retinas and compared them with existing records. A light blinked green. A similar action was performed with his right thumb and a similar green acknowledgment appeared. Janas pulled Franken back, then pushed him away. The injured man fell to his knees and whimpered through his broken teeth.

Robert Janas felt a sickness in his stomach and asked himself if this were the kind of victory for which he had hoped. He bit his lip and moved aside so that another man could repeat the actions with Bilthor Franken.

Seconds—or was it hours?—later, a cry went up: "Accepted! The computer's been programmed."

Jarl Emmett quickly placed tape reels onto the computer players, fed the leaders across the playback heads and onto pickup reels. Then he depressed a button and the tapes began to spin.

"Tell tne warship that we're surrendering," Janas called to Juan Kai. "Now!"

The engineer bent to his task, acknowledging the warship's command, saying that they would come out unarmed and surrender to the Pinkers who encircled the building.

Jarl Emmett watched the computer's boards for a few moments, then turned to Janas.

"It's done, Bob," he said slowly. "The computer has signaled Luna."

Janas nodded, slowly turned, took an energy rifle from one of the Operations men who stood guarding the Franken brothers.

"Everyone stand clear," he said, raising the rifle and aiming at the computer banks. "We'd better make sure that they don't have the facilities for recalling those orders before the message capsules are launched."

Electric flame shot across the room as the seventh-level energy beam tore into the diodes and ferrite cores, into the circuit modules and inductors—the computer screamed in the fury of its dying, but it died, quickly and terribly.

Robert Janas staggered out of the room, coughing with the acrid smoke, and boarded an undamaged elevator behind Jarl Emmett. A few moments later they reached the surface levels and crossed the Operations building main lobby. At the door they were met by the Pinkers who placed them under arrest.

Chapter XXVI

The uneasiness felt by the commander of the Solar Trading Company Patrol Ship Number 438 grew as the time for breaking out of Non-space approached. Within a few minutes his ship, along with the thirty-four other patrol ships and the two STC cruisers that now formed Battle Group IV, would return to normal space some one thousand diameters from Sol and then drive toward Earth, toward battle. But the PS 438's commander had no desire to fight, at least not in this war, not against the rebels whom he knew had something of justice on their side. But fight he must, despite his fears and reservations, for he was a man loyal to his commitments.

Standing on the bridge of his small craft, the commander of STCPS 438 was one of the first men in Battle Group IV to know of the approach of the message capsule. A blip appeared on the laser-radar, a blip that had been preceded by less than a second by a coded radio signal, broadcast widely, powerfully through Non-space. The signal was a high priority STC contact code.

Recognizing the code PS 438's computer replied, sending out another coded signal, one that was the proper reply to the capsule's broadcast. Since the PS 438's reply preceded that of its companions by a sizable fraction of a second, the capsule homed in toward that ship.

A tractor beam captured the capsule when it was within range and pulled it to the patrol craft, while the capsule's computer disarmed its destruct mechanism. Within five minutes of its detection the tape from the message capsule was brought to the commander of the PS 438. He placed the tape on a playback unit, depressed the operating switch.

"Pursuant to Executive Orders 91827-4738, dated this date, October 12, 979 FE, signed by Altho Franken, President, Bilthor Franken, Vice President Operations, Operations Division HQ, STC Central, Flagstaff Complex Division, North America (see addendum), all Solar Trading Company craft now enroute to the vicinity of Earth charged with aiding the forces of the Terran Federation under Executive Orders 91807-4734, dated October 8, 979 FE, are hereby released from those orders, repeat, *released* from those orders, and are directed to return to their bases of origin where possible. No action will be taken to aid the Terran Federation in any way outside of normal trading as specified in Solar Trading Company Regulations, Volume One, Section VI, nor to aid the forces in rebellion to it. Orders concerning further disposition of Solar Trading Company craft and personnel will be forthcoming. Signed, Jarl Emmett, Operations Supervisor, Operations Division, STC Central, Flagstaff Complex Division, North America."

There followed a complete text of the Executive Orders refered to in the message. The commander of PS 438 did not play them. It wasn't necessary.

The information was relayed to the other ships that composed Battle Group IV, and by the very nature of the orders, Battle Group IV ceased to exist.

The commander of PS 438 ordered his ship to make a 180° turn, swing back and accelerate toward the

Rim. They would go back to Loki, if they could, and await the outcome of the war. He sighed with relief and wondered why Altho Franken had changed his mind.

&

Later, much later, military experts reviewing the last battle of the Great Rebellion, or the Collapse, as it came to be called, said that the intervention of the Solar Trading Company would have had little real effect on the outcome of the Battle of Earth. The forces and military tactics of the Alliance of Independent Worlds had been too superior to what was left of the Terran Federation's defenses.

When the rebels swept toward Earth, driving before them the remnants of the Federation armada, a maser signal was transmitted from the Solar Trading Company Central Operations Division, near Flagstaff, North America. The signal was received by the STC Lunar Complex and fed into the main computer there. The master computer on Luna digested the information, determined that emergency corporate policy modifications were in effect, determined that orders implementing those modifications were valid, and set out to fulfill those orders. Within seconds of reception of that original intelligence, one of the most powerful maser transmitters in the Solar System was recalling all Solar Trading Company ships within range of its signals. At the same time Non-space message capsules were prepared, carried high above the plane of the ecliptic, out to a distance equal to the orbit of Saturn, pushed through Jump Units into Non-space, and sent toward the probable positions of the STC ships coming to the aid of the Federation. The message capsules found most of them—and they turned back, most of them, and did not join in the defense of the Federation's capital.

When the rebel fleet swept into the Solar System they found little resistance outside the orbit of Mars. The Federation had drawn back and had mounted their first line of defense only twelve million kilometers from Earth. The rebels brushed through the pickets, met the Federation's defense line, and this, the last battle, was on.

The commanders of the Federation forces had not anticipated holding the first or even the second line of defense. Their plan had been to delay the arrival of the rebels to Luna's orbit and there launch their real counteroffensive. The plan did not work; the Alliance refused to be delayed; the Federation was not ready when the rebels reached Luna, swept down across her surface, blasting the Federation strongholds, smashing the ships and men who were there to stop them. A portion of the ring wall surrounding Copernicus Crater was destroyed by a thermonuclear fireball whose ground zero point was the Federation Outpost in that crater. Along with Federation installations the STC Lunar Complex received major, though "accidental" damage, making it impossible for further messages to be sent to the Solar Trading Company ships that had now turned their backs on the Federation.

With the Lunar defense line broken the Federation fell back toward Earth herself, orbiting not far outside her atmosphere, and there brought into play the dreaded Orbital Forts, which experts had said would stop any force, no matter how strong, that attempted an invasion of the home world. The Orbital Forts, huge, hulking, weapon-studded spheres of metal, *did* delay the enemy, did scatter and thin his ranks, but they did not stop him. One by one the Orbital Forts were destroyed and the remnants of their wrecks plunged, flaming, into Earth's atmosphere.

The Federation commanders, those few who still lived, for among the dead were Grand Admiral Abli Juliene and the Chief of Staff himself, threw up their hands, ordered retreat, and Earth herself, as yet undamaged, lay below General Kantralas and his battered, bloody, decimated, but victorious rebel forces.

The Alliance of Independent Worlds starship *Guadalcanal*, the flagship of General Kantralas, met no resistance as it cut down through the atmosphere, spiraling around the planet, and finally sweeping in low across the European continent. The transmitters of the *Guadalcanal* beamed toward the city of Geneva, demanding the immediate surrender of the Federation. Geneva replied that the Chairman of the Federation could not be located, that he had vanished during the battle, but that the Vice Chairman, supported by a hastily assembled Parliament, would agree to discuss terms with the General.

When General Kantralas landed in Geneva, the Terran Federation, for all practical purposes, was dead.

Chapter XXVII

Uneasily Robert Janas stepped from the helicopter onto the roof deck of the great office building in the heart of STC Central. He looked at the needlers in the hands of the guards who greeted him, but the weapons no longer disturbed him. He had seen too many of them pointed in his direction during the past few days to give him much concern any more.

Jarl Emmett, dressed like Janas in dull prison gray, climbed from the copter and stood beside him. The helicopter's commander offered a receipt to the senior of the Pinker guards, who accepted it, signed his name, and took command of the two prisoners.

"Come this way, please," the Pinker captain said politely, gesturing toward the escalator that lead down into the STC president's suite of offices. Janas and Emmett obeyed.

A few moments later the two prisoners and their guard detail marched into the large, plush office of the president of the Solar Trading Company. Altho Franken sat behind the desk, his face strangely void of expression, his jaw whole again but somehow looking oddly misshapen. There was a needle pistol on the desk in front of him.

Milton Anchor, open hatred on his face, stood across the room. On his hip he wore a pistol similar to the one on Franken's desk. There were also four guards, wearing the presidential arm band, standing in the room; they too carried needlers.

The Pinker captain stopped before the president's desk, snapped a quasi-military salute, and said: "The prisoners Janas and Emmett, Citizen Franken."

"Thank you, captain," Franken said. "I'll take over."

The Pinker captain saluted again, turned and lead his detail back to the 'copter deck.

There was silence in Franken's office for a long while.

"Do you have any idea why you're here?" Franken

asked at last, his words slow as if his jaw still caused him pain.

"I have a few ideas," Janas answered.

"They're wrong," Franken said coldly.

"I'm surprised we're still alive," Jarl Emmett said. Franken replied with a cold, fish-like stare.

"Sit down," he said a few moments later. "And be quiet. You'll learn soon enough." He did not look at the two men again but fumbled with papers on his desk, making a great show of being busy.

Janas dropped wearily into a nearby chair. He glanced once at the armed guards, looked at Emmett, and then rested his eyes on the floor.

Some had survived, he told himself, but not many. Not enough of the Federation had survived to hold off the rebels, and just enough of the forces of the Alliance of Independent Worlds had survived to claim victory and dictate terms—but nearly a hundred and forty years of war had bled mankind white, had left him exhausted.

And Robert Janas and Jarl Emmett had survived, but perhaps only because they had surrendered to the STC Pinkers rather than being captured by Federation soldiers, and how much longer they might survive was a subject on which he did not wish to dwell. Paul D'Lugan had not survived, nor had Hal Danser —he had died on the floor at the base of the elevator shaft with a .45 caliber slug in his stomach. Juan Kai had died, too, making a foolish attempt to escape outside the Operations building. Syble Dian had not survived—an energy blast from a Pinker helicopter had cut her down on the Operations roof deck while Janas fought with Danser. Rinni and Gray, Rod Campbell, Admiral Juliene . . . only God Himself knew how many more, they had not survived, they had died as the Federation made its last, foolish, and, in a way, valiant attempt to survive.

Maura Biela had survived, had gone to the STC prison with Janas and Emmett, but rumor had it that she had been released into the custody of a rebel officer, a distant cousin or something.

As for Enid, Janas was not sure. He hoped—he believed—that she was alive. He was sure that Franken's men had not found her, for if they had Altho would surely have used her as a means of punishment. And he did not believe that there was enough of the Federation left to concern itself with a relatively unimportant girl. No, he thought, Enid is safe, as safe as anyone in the Spiral Arm.

And now it's over, he told himself for the thousandth time, over and done with, and whatever happens can't change things.

The STC has survived and that's what really matters. It can endure.

More than just the battles are over, he told himself. The whole Federation is gone, dead, and another phase of history has ended, for better or worse, and there is no changing that fact. The wheel has turned another cycle and a dark age is coming. It has happened before and it will probably happen again, and maybe there's nothing that anyone can do to alter that fact either.

Rome, so long ago, four thousand years ago, had begun as a kingdom, then became a republic. It had grown in wealth and power, had spread out to conquer and civilize the world—and ultimately it had fallen. Darkness had come after it, ages of barbarism and superstition, and at last something had grown from it. The knowledge and wisdom of Rome had not died with it, not quite. Before Rome fell it had spread fertile seeds that centuries later sprouted—Britain, Gaul, Hispania. Western Civilization had sprung from the ruins of Rome, as Rome had sprung from the ruins of the Etruscans and the Greeks, as the Greeks had sprung from the ruins of the Mycenaeans. Out of the ruins of Rome a technological civilization had grown such as none the world had seen before, a civilization with its faults and weaknesses, with its superstitions and ignorances, but one that believed in freedom and honor and a rational, inquiring mind; one that reached for the stars.

It, too, had died, had grown weak and decadent; had lost its dreams and fallen into darkness before the barbarian hordes. Out of that darkness, out of more decades of barbarism, had risen still another civilization, a planet-wide society that remembered and honored the heritage of the West, that climbed again for the stars—and reached them. *Terran* civilization had broken the barriers that held Man shackled to his tiny system of worlds and had given him the galaxy. The Solar Trading Company had played a great part in that conquest—and perhaps it was the true heir of the West.

Now the Terran Federation, having spread across the worlds of a thousand stars, having breathed into them the life and mind of mankind, had grown corrupt, had violated its heritage, and its day upon the stage of history was past. It too had come to an end.

So the darkness came once again, swallowing up the past. But the heritage would not die in the darkness. The genius of Man to rise phoenix-like from his own destruction would keep alive this heritage, and one day—not a century, perhaps not even five centuries, perhaps ten centuries from now—it would rise again, build again, conquer itself and the universe that opposed it.

Perhaps there was nothing Robert Janas or any other man could do to stop *that* inexorable march of history. Perhaps *it was so* and nothing could be done to change it, nothing now. But—and this was his hope, his prayer, the dream on which he had staked his life—but perhaps the Solar Trading Company could survive the darkness, could endure, could keep commerce alive between the stars while darkness lay across Man's Spiral Arm, could carry a spark of life, the trade of ideas and goods, between the stars so that men would know that there were still other worlds and other men, so that the darkness would be shorter and less intolerable.

He did not know. He could only hope.

And he was too realistic a man to think that he could determine or even predict how men would live fifty generations hence. That determination was left to his descendants, but he believed, as he looked back across Man's chaotic, glorious history, that a better world would arise than the one in which he had lived. Maybe men could never reach perfection, whatever that was, he told himself, but it was to Man's everlasting glory that he did not cease to try, that he kept on dreaming and kept on battling to see that his dreams came to fruition.

Janas remembered a line from an ancient poem, written back before the ships from Earth had climbed toward the stars, and it went something like this: "Each age is a dream that is dying, or one that is coming to birth."

So it was with Janas' age. A dream was dying, was dead, but the next age, the one that followed his, would be one that was coming to birth. And that was sufficient.

There was a buzz from the communicator in Altho Franken's desk. The president of the Solar Trading Company jumped, then bent forward to stab the button.

"Yes," he said in a hoarse voice.

"Citizen Altho Franken?" asked a voice from the communicator.

"Yes, it is," Franken said. Janas saw Franken's hand shake as he reached for a cigar.

"General Henri Kantralas calling."

"Put him on," Franken said, taking a deep breath.

"Citizen Franken?" came a deep, booming voice from the communicator.

Janas wished that he could see the recessed screen and the face of the man who had beaten the Federation.

Franken nodded.

"Allow me to congratulate you, Citizen Franken," the general's voice said. "You showed great wisdom in maintaining the Solar Trading Company's neutrality."

Franken said, "Thank you, general."

"Let me come straight to the point, citizen."

"P-please do, general," Franken stammered, and looked up at Janas.

"I had my aide arrange this call for a specific reason, Citizen Franken," the general went on. "The STC is the only recognized neutral body left. Both myself and the Acting Chairman have agreed that we would like the Solar Trading Company to act as an impartial go-between and witness during our negotiations. Is the Solar Trading Company willing to carry out this function?"

"Why, yes, general," Franken said, something like relief coming across his face.

"Very good," General Kantralas said. He paused for a moment. "Two of your employees have been highly recommended to me. May I suggest that you appoint them as your agents?"

Franken looked at Janas, then at Emmett, puzzlement on his face. "Please do, general," he said after a while, his voice hesitant and reserved.

"Thank you, citizen," the general's voice said pleasantly. "You have a—" He paused for a moment. "—a Captain Robert Janas and a Citizen Jarl Emmett in your employ, I believe. My aide suggested that they be present at this conversation."

"But, general," Franken almost yelled, "these men are criminals. They're re ..."

"Citizen Franken," Kantralas said, his voice suddenly hard and firm, "I am sure that you are well aware of the joint amnesty issued by both the Alliance and the Federation. This amnesty covers *all* persons involved in the so-called Rebellion, on either side, except for a few *war* criminals."

"General ..." Franken tried to speak.

"Perhaps you do not feel that these gentlemen are covered by the amnesty, citizen. Surely they can't be considered war criminals."

"Well," Franken said, "I don't see ..."

"Perhaps you would care to try their cases in a court of law?" The general's voice held a subdued threat.

"No, general," Franken said. "Of course not."

"Very good. Are they present?"

"Yes," Franken said with a sigh, gesturing for Janas

and Emmett to come behind the desk so that they could see the general's face in the 3-V and be seen by him.

"Good afternoon, gentlemen," the general said. "Are you willing to serve in this capacity?"

"Very willing, sir," Janas answered for both of them, looking into the deep eyes of that man who somehow reminded him of Michelangelo's *Moses*.

"Would you please come to Geneva at your earliest convenience?" General Kantralas asked.

While Franken stammered affirmative replies for them, and Milton Anchor glared in anger, Janas exchanged puzzled looks with Emmett. Each replied with a shrug. They did not know how much Kantralas knew of them, but it was enough. They were grateful.

Janas turned as Franken concluded his conversation with the general and looked out through the window into the darkening sky, a sky where, one after another, stars were beginning to show, a sky filling with the stars that were Man's inheritance.

The death pangs of the old civilization were not over yet, he thought, and probably would not be over within his lifetime. And he would never live to see the birth pangs of the next. But so be it.

Out There, in that inverted bowl of stars, mankind and his strange, sometimes paradoxical civilization would go on—but to what?

the end

A Selection of Legend Titles

Prices and other details are liable to change

ARROW BOOKS, BOOKSERVICE BY POST, PO BOX 29, DOUGLAS, ISLE OF MAN, BRITISH ISLES

NAME...

ADDRESS..

....

....

Please enclose a cheque or postal order made out to Arrow Books Ltd. for the amount due and allow the following for postage and packing.

U.K. CUSTOMERS: Please allow 22p per book to a maximum of £3.00.

B.F.P.O. & EIRE: Please allow 22p per book to a maximum of £3.00

OVERSEAS CUSTOMERS: Please allow 22p per book.

Whilst every effort is made to keep prices low it is sometimes necessary to increase cover prices at short notice. Arrow Books reserve the right to show new retail prices on covers which may differ from those previously advertised in the text or elsewhere.

Bestselling SF/Horror

☐ The Labyrinth	Robert Faulcon	£2.50
☐ Night Train	Thomas F. Monteleone	£2.50
☐ Malleus Maleficarum	Montague Summers	£4.50
☐ The Devil Rides Out	Dennis Wheatley	£2.50
☐ The Shadow of the Torturer	Gene Wolfe	£2.95
☐ Contact	Carl Sagan	£3.50
☐ Cobra Strike (Venture SF 17)	Timothy Zahn	£2.95
☐ Night Visions	Campbell, Barker, Tuttle	£2.95
☐ Bones of the Moon	Jonathan Carroll	£2.50
☐ The Island	Guy N. Smith	£2.50
☐ The Hungry Moon	Ramsey Campbell	£2.95
☐ Pin	Andrew Neiderman	£1.50

Prices and other details are liable to change

ARROW BOOKS, BOOKSERVICE BY POST, PO BOX 29, DOUGLAS, ISLE OF MAN, BRITISH ISLES

NAME . . . .

ADDRESS . . . .

. . . .

. . . .

Please enclose a cheque or postal order made out to Arrow Books Ltd. for the amount due and allow the following for postage and packing.

U.K. CUSTOMERS: Please allow 22p per book to a maximum of £3.00.

B.F.P.O. & EIRE: Please allow 22p per book to a maximum of £3.00

OVERSEAS CUSTOMERS: Please allow 22p per book.

Whilst every effort is made to keep prices low it is sometimes necessary to increase cover prices at short notice. Arrow Books reserve the right to show new retail prices on covers which may differ from those previously advertised in the text or elsewhere.